"*Never Lost* beautifully captures the connection between family, nature, and survival. Reading it brought back memories of the summers I spent with my grandmother in Yosemite, where we honored the land in the same way the characters do."

—Elmer Winfree, Elder of the Mono Tribe

AARON C. ANDERSON

NEVER LOST

Helping talented writers publish exceptional books

This is a work of fiction. References to real people, events, establishments, organizations, or locales are intended only to provide a sense of authenticity and are used fictitiously. All other characters, and all incidents and dialogue are drawn from the author's imagination and are not to be construed as real.

Never Lost

Copyright © 2025 Aaron C. Anderson. All rights reserved.

Printed in the United States of America. For information, address Acorn Publishing, LLC
3943 Irvine Blvd. Ste. 218, Irvine, CA 92602

www.acornpublishingllc.com

Interior design by Nico Seidita
Cover design by Damonza

Anti-Piracy Warning: The unauthorized reproduction or distribution of copyrighted work is illegal. Criminal copyright infringement, including infringement without monetary gain, is investigated by the FBI and is punishable by up to five years in federal prison and a fine of $250,000.

All rights reserved. No part of this book may be used or reproduced in any manner whatsoever, including Internet usage, without written permission from the author.

ISBN-13: 9798885281287 (paperback)
Library of Congress Control Number: 2025905699

DEDICATION

To my fine sons Erik and Ian. For the many adventures we have shared.

Author's Note

The moments that define us are scattered through the routine of uneventful days. These impressions leave a photo history in our minds and a guideline of ethics and understanding that propel us along our life's path. In some families, this is a shared journey from generation to generation, never ending.

ONE

Zane listened until the room came fully into focus. The waxing moon cast a dim light through the clutter of clothes and bedding. He placed his feet onto the cold wood floor. With his bare arm, he pushed the condensation from the window, sending rivulets of water coursing into puddles on the wooden ledge.

He scanned the moonlit junipers and scrub brush that sent dark shadows onto the patchy grass of a yard. Stroking his long black hair from his face, he looked at the clock and decided to let Sara sleep awhile longer. The floor of the drafty old house squeaked as he walked down the hall to the living room.

After feeding some dry pine into the wood stove and blowing life into the last glowing embers, he reluctantly stepped into a cold shower. The icy water shocked his muscles, chasing the last vestige of sleep from his oak solid body. As he dried and dressed, he heard Sara picking up the house as she worked her way toward the kitchen.

The peaceful routine of the morning thinly veiled the tension, heavy in the room. Today would be the beginning of an extraordinary adventure for Zane and Sara's sons. It had taken them thirteen years to come to this moment. Zane was responsible for the education of his sons. During his youth, his grandfather had given him a knowledge that few men shared. Most of the lessons were basic life skills like patience or respecting your elders and the world around you. But some took him into isolated and foreboding places where he learned to deal with difficult and sometimes desperate situations.

Sara did not share his dream for their sons. Learning the skills and traditions of their father's tribe was never part of her plan. She thought it was not reasonable for her young sons to be subjected to the hardships that Zane proposed. Every year there were news stories of grown men, who went missing while hunting and were later found dead from exposure. Her sons were just children.

Through the years Sara endured and adapted as much as she could to the cultural differences in the raising of their children. She had been naïve to the hardships of an intercultural marriage, but she loved Zane. She also knew there was no better teacher than Zane. He would not be careless with their sons. The boys had been hunting and fishing since they were little children. Their time in the woods with their father and his friends was as natural to them as spending time playing baseball was to other boys. No matter her objections, Sara felt she could not deny her sons their father's heritage and she'd given her consent.

The frost crunched under Zane's feet as he went to stow gear in the truck. A tall jackrabbit watched him work from his perch in the middle of the long gravel driveway. The approaching dawn pressed the cold closer to the earth, and Zane warmed his hands in his pockets. The boys' bikes were lying in the yard and the archery target with their practice arrows scattered across it was tucked into the edge of the buck brush. His sons were still boys, but they were ready to start moving in a direction that would take them to their place amongst the men.

This would be the first time Zane would let them reach out as far as they dared. They would make decisions that resulted in real consequences. He had faith in his sons, but he knew that they would be exposed, and anything could happen. If they made a wrong choice, he may not be able to save them.

The fear of losing one of his sons swelled as a sick pain in the hollow of his gut. The danger was real, but Zane knew that going was the only way to find out if his sons were ready for a survival trip in the high timber. The lessons he learned when his grandfather had taken him to search for his place in the world spoke to him every day.

The skills and knowledge are a sacred trust, Zane thought. "If I don't teach my sons, the wisdom of my grandfather will be lost to The People."

Zane knew the hearts of his sons. He knew they were strong in the spirit and excited for the challenge. He prayed every day that the spirits of their ancestors would protect them, and the mountains would call to them. Zane, committed to their education, believed in his heart that they would embrace whatever lay ahead and see it through to the other side. They were ready.

Two

Zane turned on the light in his sons' room. "Come on, guys. Time to get up."

Springing to life, the two sinewy, long-haired boys pitched themselves from their beds and started pulling on their clothes.

Zane took another load to the truck then checked his list. He had packed almost everything the night before, after the boys had gone to bed. In addition to the regular camping equipment, Zane included leather clothes and boots that he had made. They had taken him weeks to cut and hand stitch. He had worked on them after the boys were asleep, so they would be a surprise.

The boots were his design. They were thick enough to protect against snake bites, and snug enough to give good support and a comfortable walk. The pants and breech clouts were traditional Nez Perce. They were made from hides from past hunts, including the deer that the boys had shot last fall.

Joseph pulled on a black T-shirt and sweatshirt and then pushed his hair out of his face.

"Ty, what do you think Dad's going to let us take? A survival trip in the mountains is going to be cold. Do you think we can bring our pack boots?"

"I hope we don't need them," Ty said. "I hope I get a pair of boots like Dad's."

Joseph thought his father would probably let them wear their packs. He wanted the leather boots, too, but he really would rather have warm, dry feet, and he knew he could trust his packs if they were going into the snow.

"I'm taking my normal stuff. Unless Dad says I can't."

"Me, too, then, but I sure hope I get a pair of Dad's boots."

"Boys, you'd better hurry up," Sara said as she walked into their room. "Your father is about ready to go. What do you want for breakfast?"

"Cereal," Ty said.

"Same for me," agreed Joseph.

"Well, if that is what you want. But I'm making bacon, potatoes, and eggs for your father. You guys hurry up. You know how anxious your father gets when he is ready to go. I think he is in one of his 'we're outta here' moods," Sara said as she returned to the kitchen to prepare breakfast.

Sara was busy working when Zane wandered into the kitchen. "That smells great, sweetheart." He filled his salt container and slipped it into a leather pouch.

"You take care of my babies," Sara said, tears in her eyes.

"The boys will be fine." Zane kissed and held his wife. "We will be out of touch for about two weeks. I'll call you as soon as we get out. The maps I left on my desk show exactly where we'll be, and how we plan to walk out. I'll have the pilot call if we need to make any last-minute changes in plans."

"Pilot," Ty said, walking into the kitchen. "Joseph," he yelled, "we're going to fly in!"

Joseph trotted into the kitchen. "Cool. Where are we going? Alaska?"

"You'll know soon enough," Zane said, winking at Sara to reassure her. "Now, eat your breakfast and kiss your mom good-bye. We need to get rolling."

THREE

From Bend, Oregon to the Idaho border was about a four-hour drive. Zane loved every mile. The memory of wild Oregon filled his mind. Most of his life, he had hiked and hunted this beautiful country. Every foot of it either brought forth great memories of past trips or the promise of a new adventure.

As they drove through Vale at the Idaho border, Zane remembered the great pheasant hunts of his childhood. It was different now. Only rich city boys could hunt here. Trying to hold onto their land in hard financial times, the local farmers and ranchers had sold the hunting rights to their fields. Even their own sons couldn't hunt there any longer.

After a few years, the wild birds learned that they could find sanctuary from the local hunters in the fields leased to the out-of-towners. The people who leased the hunting rights seldom showed. The overcrowded birds developed diseases, and the wild pheasants nearly died out. Now, the farmers stocked the fields with pen-raised birds they released in the mornings when the hunters showed up. Nice, slow, chicken-like pheasants. Even city boys could hit them.

Civilization comes to the country, Zane thought as he drove across the border into Idaho. Idaho is a wonderful state. Like Oregon, it cares for its wild areas with the same regard as it cares for its people.

By late afternoon, they headed northeast along the Lochsa River. The sweet crisp smell of spring rushed through the open windows of the truck. Warmth radiated through the windshield and the stiff ride of the old Ford Bronco rocked them down the road with daydreams of good days ahead. Beside them, the river crashed and rolled through the canyon.

"Boys," Zane said, "look at this world around us. God lives here."

Ty couldn't believe this was happening. He was out of school a month early. It meant he would need to attend summer school, but for only three weeks. Today, he was free and on his way to another adventure. When he laid back and thought about the outstanding moments of his life, the trips with his dad were his best memories. Even back when he was three years old, he would ride on his father's shoulders while they hunted for rabbits.

Hunting and fishing meant something new and exciting around every turn, and Ty couldn't get enough of it. He already knew he wanted to be a hunting guide when he grew up. That way, he and Dad could go on trips whenever they wanted. Joseph would come, but he didn't really like the kill that much. He liked to fish, though, and he could track an animal almost as good as Dad.

Ty hoped that one day he would be able to see the slight disturbances on the trails and know what they meant like Joseph could. But he had his skills and knew that he would be a better hunter than Joseph when they got older. Ty knew he wanted it more than Joseph.

He didn't always understand Joseph's thinking, but he loved

his big brother and was always proud of him. On this trip, Ty was not just relieved; he was thrilled to have Joseph along. This was not like other hunting trips. Dad had talked about past survival trips; long frozen days survived only because of marathon walks with little to no food. He would need Joseph's help if Dad left them alone. Ty would never admit it, but the thought of being really alone in a remote place filled him with a fear that made his stomach lurch into his throat.

Zane pulled over and stopped. "We'll camp here tonight, guys."

"Yes! Get me out of this truck!" Ty said as he and Joseph piled out into the gravel parking area above the river.

"Hallelujah, I've been wanting out all day! What's this place famous for?" Joseph asked, walking toward a bronze plaque mounted into an overgrown stone monument.

"There is a hot spring one-quarter of a mile up the trail on the other side of the river. It's called Jerry Johnson Hot Springs. The local people have been using it for thousands of years. It is one of my favorite places. You guys are going to love it. All you need is sleeping bags; I'll get everything else. If you want to fish, get your poles and tackle. They are behind the seat. If you guys get lucky, keep enough for breakfast. We already have food for dinner."

The boys ran across the narrow bridge over the churning water and stashed their sleeping bags in the brush next to the trail. With only an hour or so before dark, they wanted to get down to the river.

Zane loaded his pack and headed toward the trail. "Don't wade into the river, boys. It has a stronger current than you might think."

Zane followed the well-worn trail along the creek toward the springs. Deep in the canyon the long shadows weaved into a cool carpet of damp earth. Zane enjoyed the solitude of the lonesome afternoon shade.

. . .

Joseph and Ty went straight down to the water's edge. It was a beautiful sun-soaked late afternoon. The glare washed up the turbulent rushing current, giving a deceptively warm glow to the icy cold water. Joseph quickly scooted along the bank, turning over rocks to determine what insects the fish were currently feeding on.

"We don't have time for that," Ty said. "I'm going to use my black and gold Panther Martin."

"Suit yourself, that should work fine, but I want to use some kind of a fly. I think I'll use a rubber-legs followed by a black AP," Joseph said, rummaging through his flies as he walked up along the bank. "We better stick together even though you're using a lure, okay?"

"Sounds fine to me." Ty preferred to stick together. A couple of years ago, he had fallen into a river a lot like this one. Dad had to jump in after him. They had lost a whole bunch of gear, including Ty's new fishing rod. It had scared him badly. When he hit the water, it took his breath away.

He'd tried to swim, but the river's bubbly mouth slipped up over his legs and, almost gently, swallowed him under. Then, as he bounced along, looking helplessly up through the foam at a distorted image of a bush limb reaching out over the water, his father's strong hand had seized his shoulder and pulled him up into the air. He never wanted to experience that hollow, lost, helpless feeling again. Joseph could stay as close to him as he wanted.

Joseph and Ty walked upstream. They weren't the first people to fish in this stretch of the river this year. They could see the old worm containers and discarded fishing line, left by uncaring people. Their father had told them that these people suffered from a cultural disorder that made them think everywhere they went was a garbage dump, that life possessed no value and that wild things were just for killing.

Two hundred yards upstream, they saw a giant old fir tree that had fallen out into the river. The water's patient caress had pulled away the supporting earth, felling the regal giant. The branches now provided shade and diverted the relentless current into a swirling eddy for fish to rest from the constant press of the river.

"This is where the fish live," said Joseph. "I'm going over to above this tree and drift under it."

"Go ahead. Do you think I'll spoil your drift if I cast out from here?"

"No, go ahead. But you know what I'd do if I were you? I'd walk down that tree, find a safe place to sit down so you won't fall off, then cast in toward the bank."

"I don't know if I want to," Ty started.

"If you're scared, I'll go out there with you," Joseph cut in.

"No, I'm not scared. I can do it."

Ty was scared, but he wasn't going to let Joseph know how ominous the turbulent black eddy looked to him. He also knew that if Joseph said the fishing was best away from the bank, chances were good he should fish away from the bank.

Ty put down his small tackle box and carefully climbed past the rocks that had anchored the seventy-foot white fir into the cut bank above the water. The tree was a good three feet across where it had sprouted from the earth. With the bank another six feet high, Ty was looking at ten feet to the water. He glanced over and saw Joseph waiting to make sure he was all right. Branches pulling against the current gave rhythmic sway to Ty's bridge out into the water. The pulse was a constant reminder that one day this river would have its way, and this great fir would succumb to its desire that everything join its quest to reach the ocean.

Ty went fifty feet or so to where the trunk was one and a half feet across and still a little way above the water. The branches and top of the tree that rested in the water balanced and gave support from the current. Once Ty settled in, he felt quite comfortable. There were limbs to hold onto if he needed them and even one to lean back against.

Ty looked up to let Joseph know that he was all set, but

Joseph was busy drifting his line under the log Ty had crawled down.

Joseph had waited until Ty was halfway down the tree and moving comfortably, then he walked upstream to where he could get a good drift under the tree. Joseph had a spinning rod with a six-pound test line. From the end of his line, he rigged on a four-foot long 4X fluorocarbon leader to a split shot, with a fourteen-inch leader to his rubber legs, then a 12-inch leader to his AP.

Casting out to about twenty feet above the log, he watched his fly dip gently with the current under the log. His fly flowed with the current until it reached the shadow of the tree on the water, then suddenly with a shock and a lurch his pole sprang to life. An eighteen-inch brown trout swallowed the nymph and made a run for the underwater tangle of branches. Joseph didn't have to set the hook. The fish hit the fly so hard, Joseph knew he had him.

He held tension on the line as the fish pulled toward the fast water. It was the best fighting fish of his life. Running upstream, it took line and cleared the water three times before he managed to get it to the bank. It was the biggest trout he had ever caught. Joseph shouted in victory. He put his finger through the fish's gills and held it up for Ty to see. Ty couldn't look, he had one on himself.

Ty saw Joseph with a fish on and thought, *Man, I should have used a fly like Joseph.* Looking up the log and realizing he had no time to make a change before dark, he settled down and cast up to about three feet from the bank and started reeling in. The lure hadn't traveled ten feet when a twisting weight surged against his line. A hungry brown trout had attacked his lure and was headed for deep water. The fight was on! Ty struggled to stay on the log while battling the fish.

The powerful underwater predator tried every trick to tangle the line or spit the hook. He ran for the heavy current then swept downstream, but Ty pulled him back to the eddy line. The thick bodied trout then ran toward Ty, trying to twist the hook out of his mouth, but Ty reeled fast and held tension. When the fight ended, Ty held up a sixteen-inch brown trout. Grinning from ear-to-ear, Joseph and Ty gave each other a thumbs up. Then, as quickly as they could, they cast in again to hook up a couple more.

FOUR

Zane stood at the edge of the trees, closed his eyes and soaked in the smells of the conifers and the sound of the gentle sway of the aspen in the evening breeze. The trail was a peaceful walk along a small creek overhung with forest canopy that led to a suddenly open meadow with wisps of steam drifting up from the grass and rock. The hot mineral springs percolated up through the earth in wide marshy patches that trickled slowly to the creek.

He walked to the far side of the meadow and down to the creek to his favorite camp area. He was the first person into this spot this season and the winter had pressed hard on the land. The fire ring was washed out and tree branches lay tangled after being dragged down by the heavy snow and wind.

Zane prepared a level sleeping area free of rocks and debris, then laid out the ground covers for the sleeping bags. He gathered the firewood, made roasting sticks out of willow branches, then went to work repairing winter damage on one of the central pools. The hot springs had been used by the Native People for thousands of years. This had always been a place of peace and healing.

The People would travel to these mineral baths and respect it as neutral ground where there was truce between all who rested here. The healing water rose up from the ground and mixed with the fresh clear stream. Year after year the areas where the hot springs poured up from the ground, the cool creek was mixed in to a desired temperature.

Pools were made by stacking the river rock as deep as someone was willing to work. By the end of the summer, some of the pools had been improved by hundreds of people till they became as comfortable as any hot tub. Zane waded barefoot into the icy water and started moving rocks. The spring runoff had overrun the pools, scattering the rocks so there were only impressions where deep pools had once been. As the wall of rocks diverted the main thrust of the creek around the hot water rising from below, the water warmed, and the work became more pleasant. It took an hour before they could enjoy a warm soak.

A half hour after dark, Joseph and Ty trotted up to Zane's once peaceful fire. The two young men, drunk with adventure, proudly held their trophies aloft.

"That was the best fishing I've ever done!" Joseph said.

Ty yelled, "Look what I caught!" He held up the beautiful native trout.

"We kept three. One for each of us," Joseph said. "But I bet we threw back five or six. It was the best! Can we stop back here on our way home?"

"Depends how things go, but at this point I kind of doubt it. Don't worry; this is one of my favorite places. We'll be back, but right now let's cook up these nice elk steaks. Here are some baked potatoes. I cooked them last night. We will warm them by the fire. You guys watch your own, okay?"

"I always burn my potatoes. Can you do mine?" asked Ty. "And I want to eat my fish. I'll have my steak for breakfast. Okay?"

"Yeah, that sounds good to me," said Joseph. "I like to eat my fish before the spots fade."

"All right, we'll have fish. But I want you guys to cook your steaks. We need to make a quick start tomorrow. Get to it, if you want to take a soak before bed. I also want to fill you in on where we're going and what we'll be doing."

The boys hurried down to the creek to clean the fish. They were filled with the thrill of the catch and eager to finally learn where they were going and how they would be spending the next two weeks.

While Zane whittled on some small skewers to help hold the fish onto the roasting sticks, he thought back to the last time he was at these springs. In the pouring rain he rested in the hot water on a late August night. Lightning flashed frantically along the ridges on both sides of the creek. Zane had watched one bolt hit a tall white fir sending it into fiery fragments. The night looked like day and the thunder echoed through the canyon like cannons.

The other people at the springs had all run for cover through the sheets of water when the lightning strikes walked across the meadow. Zane had always figured that when God was ready for him, no amount of running would change his destiny. And by God, that was the finest fireworks display Zane had ever seen. He looked for thunderheads in the star-filled sky and then turned his attention to mounding the coals to roast these most beautiful brown trout.

FIVE

When he awoke, Zane looked up into the branches that draped low over their sleeping bags. He could see beyond the lowest branches. It would be light in another half hour. Zane slipped out of his bag and put on his pants. His neatly tied black hair lay to the middle of his back, the cold morning greeted him like an old friend. Zane liked the feeling of the morning dew washing across his bare feet, so he left his boots next to his sleeping bag and walked down to the creek.

Thirty years ago, an old friend of his grandfather had told him if he bathed himself in cold water every morning, his body would stay hard and sickness would never linger in his bones. From that day, he had done a cold water wash every morning. He hated it, but old wisdom had prevailed. He was seldom sick, and his strength had only increased over the years.

Knowing his friend's Coyote nature, Zane had often wondered during these icy episodes if these supposed results were only a coincidence. He wondered if the old Shoshone would be laughing if he saw Zane splashing himself with icy water on these dark and frozen mornings.

Zane thought about his grandfather almost every day of his life. His father had died in Vietnam when Zane was an infant. He and his mother lived in a small trailer on the Reservation in Lapwai, Idaho. She had never seemed to have much time for him.

If it had not been for his grandfather, he would have felt alone in the world. He had never called his grandfather by his name; he was always Grandfather, a name spoken with respect, with reverence. To Zane he was a savior from a life of lonely desperation. More than that, his grandfather, who had been both warrior and healer before the devastation of the Nez Perce way of life had taught him the skills and language of their ancestors. He also taught Zane dignity and how to treat the world with respect.

Zane was seventeen when his grandfather died. At one hundred and ten years old, Zane's grandfather was a powerful source of history for the Nez Perce Nation. He had told Zane many stories during the time they had shared. He told about life when The People lived where they had always lived throughout Northern Idaho, and about how everything changed with the "Steal Treaty" in 1870.

His grandfather told of their fight with the government soldiers and how The People ran into Montana till they got to the place the soldiers called Milk River, where they were exposed and surrounded. They could not fight without the risk of losing everyone. Only a few hundred People were left when they were sent away from their land like camp dogs. After seven years, some of The People were allowed to return to what was left of their land.

Those People promised the exiled warriors that they would never be forgotten. They would remember what had happened, and The People would never forget them. Zane couldn't imagine that a greater man had ever trod upon the earth than his grandfather.

The boys were up at first light, getting their equipment together. After everything had been cleaned up and returned to a natural state, the boys headed for the road. Zane took one final moment to feel the morning sun on his face and to enjoy the peacefulness of the valley floor.

Zane knew that the ancients honored these springs as a place of healing, free from war. It was a sanctuary of peace and comfort. Zane spread his arms wide and turned his palms open to the field. Joy spread through him like a wind crossing the grass. Zane smiled, gathered his things and then hurried to catch up to his sons.

He had told the boys that they could bring everything they had in their pockets, their hunting knives, and no more. For clothes they could take their polar fleece jackets. Zane said he had everything else. So when the boys got back to the truck, they stowed their fishing gear and sleeping bags. Then they put everything they were allowed to take into a day pack.

"This is a great spot, Dad. I want to stop on our way home," said Ty.

"Ty, this place will never be the same as it was last night. We will come back here, but don't expect things to be the same. Each day brings its own magic. If I were you, I'd never fish that same pool again," Zane said as he pulled onto the road heading toward Missoula, Montana.

Ty wasn't listening. As they drove off, he watched his tree stretching out into the ambling river. He remembered the power and run of the brown trout that had become entwined with his life the night before.

Zane and the boys ate lunch in the truck. They enjoyed the northbound journey, wending their way along the Locksha River till it turned up into the mountain divide that separated Idaho from Montana. They arrived at the small airport outside of Missoula around midday. The sandwiches the boys ate for lunch sat heavily in their stomachs, nervous with anticipation of the flight that lay ahead.

The pilot waited for them in his office. As Zane and the boys walked in, Mike stood and walked over to greet them.

"You must be Zane Carter," he said, putting out his hand. "I'm Mike Wallace."

"I'm glad to meet you in person, Mr. Wallace. Is everything ready to go?" Zane asked, shaking his hand.

"You bet, and you can call me Mike. I flew over the lake last week. We should have no problem landing. The ice has melted back far enough that I can get you right up to the shore."

"Sounds great, Mike. I'd like you to meet my boys, Joseph and Ty."

"Nice to meet you, Mr. Wallace," Joseph said, also shaking Mike's hand.

"Yeah, nice to meet you," echoed Ty. "You're going to land on a lake?"

"That's right. That's my plane right over there. The best float plane anywhere around here," Mike said. "You guys ready to go for a ride?"

"We're ready," Zane said. "Do you have someone to shuttle my truck?"

"My wife is around here somewhere. Let's stow your gear. She should show up by then."

"Let's do it, boys. Get your day packs and my black duffel. They're right on top in the back."

The boys ran out to get the bags. Zane and Mike walked toward the plane.

"Zane, this is the first time I've dropped people off with no real equipment. Most of the time, I have to tie things on the outside. Are you sure you don't want me to at least fly over after a few days, or a week, to check on you guys? I'd do it for no extra money."

"No, Mike. I'd rather we stuck to the original plan. You drop us and shuttle our truck to the lake. I would also like to leave our street clothes with you in the plane to put in the truck. I don't want the boys to have to spend the first night wet and cold if we have to wade to the shore."

"If that's the way you want it. I made up a simple form for you to sign, so if they find you later, I won't have to answer to your wife," Mike said, handing Zane a single sheet of paper from the plane.

"No problem. I appreciate you taking on the job."

Joseph and Ty ran up with the bags.

"Dad, do you want us to change here?" Ty said, eager to try on his new boots.

"We'll change our clothes after we land. Why don't you go ahead and use the restroom now. It will be your last chance for a while," Zane said.

Ty set down the duffel and headed back toward Mike's office.

"Here are your keys, Dad." Joseph tossed them to his father and ran to catch Ty.

Joseph and Ty ran back to the airport office and waiting room. They went inside and found the restroom.

"Joseph, I know Dad said only take what was in my pockets, but I hadn't put in any matches or anything. All my camping stuff was still in my bag. Do you think Dad would mind if I brought a couple of things that I was going to put in my pockets, anyway?"

"I wouldn't," Joseph said. "That would be cheating. Besides, I think Dad would know. And you know you'd feel bad about it later. Dad won't make us do anything we can't do."

"Okay, I won't. But I don't know how Dad would know. He can't see in my pockets."

Ty wished he hadn't asked. He could have at least kept the fishing equipment and matches he had slipped into his pocket. It wasn't such a big deal to Joseph, who could start a fire by striking a piece of flint with his knife. Dad could start a fire with flint, or a bow drill made from sticks.

Ty needed matches. He felt nauseous and steadied himself against the wall. He was more scared than he had previously realized. He was glad he wasn't the big brother. It was nice having Joseph there when he needed him.

When the boys left the restroom there was a lady about their mom's age waiting for them. She walked up to the boys and greeted them with a warm smile and a friendly voice. "You must be Joseph and Ty. I'm Lisa, Mike's wife. I wanted to meet you boys before you took off on your adventure. You are a couple of pretty special guys to be going on a trip like this. I know I'd never be able to survive out in these mountains. It's hard enough for Mike to get me to go hunting with him when we take our camp trailer. Well, I better get going if I'm going to get to the lake before Mike. Oh, your dad said he didn't know, but you might have some things you want me to take to the truck."

Ty turned red and looked over at Joseph. "Yeah," Ty said, reaching into his pocket and pulling a plastic baggy with some fishing line, hooks, sinkers, and matches in it. "You can take this."

"Are you sure you don't need that? I think your dad would want you to take that."

"No, you'd better take it," Ty said with a little greater resolve. "I won't need it."

"If you say so," Lisa said, sounding very impressed. "You make sure your dad calls us when you guys get out, okay?"

"Okay," Ty said, embarrassed he had thought about cheating and proud that Lisa had been impressed.

"Bye then and have fun," Lisa said as she headed out for the truck.

"Told you Dad would know," Joseph said.

Ty flushed again, and the boys trotted off to the plane.

Six

The plane roared along the narrow runway and leapt smoothly into the air. They rose fast and banked left, the angle making Ty's shoulder press into Joseph's. Mike leveled out and headed north-west.

Joseph and Ty had both flown before; but big commercial jets were quite different than this little four-seat float plane. The cabin vibrated with the turn of the propeller. The doors were thin, almost fragile, like a man could tear one off and throw it away. The windows were plastic with small crank open squares in the corner for ventilation. Ty and Joseph could feel the cold pressing through the sheet metal walls.

The little plane didn't feel like much of a safety net as the ground fell away, giving a view of an ocean of trees. Ty felt like a mouse hanging from a falcon's claw. Reaching the ground below safely seemed less and less likely the farther from the airport they flew. Ty strained to fill his mind with anything other than imminent death.

"Do we have any parachutes?" Joseph asked after a few minutes.

"Joseph," Mike said as he smiled, "I'm hurt. You don't trust me."

"Oh, I trust you all right. I just wonder if there are any parachutes."

Ty could tell Joseph was nervous. He was holding on tight to the seat and staring out the window as if looking for a place to land.

Then Ty started to shake. Not all over, first his knees, then his stomach, then his teeth. He started looking for a place to land, too.

The boys fell conspicuously quiet. Zane looked back to see how they were enjoying the ride. He loved riding in small planes, especially on warm spring days. It was an exhilarating experience, but the boys didn't look like they were having very much fun.

"Guys," Zane said, "isn't this great?"

"How long before we land, Dad?" Ty asked.

"About twenty minutes," replied Mike. "Are you boys getting sick?"

"I'm fine," Joseph said. Even as he said it, he realized he was relaxing into the idea of the small box of a plane.

"I'm okay, too," Ty said, glancing at Joseph.

Joseph looked at Ty. "I liked big planes better at first, but now I think this is kind of cool. I just hope it's not too rough when we land on the lake."

"It's not really different from landing on the ground. You stop a little faster and the water splashes up the sides of the plane. But I've never swamped yet."

Mike found it hard to sound reassuring. He flew hunters in and out during the regular hunting seasons, and he always enjoyed scaring them a little. He was trying hard not to today, but he wasn't very practiced at making people feel totally comfortable.

"You boys are doing real good back there. A lot of grown men throw up. Sometimes they even pee their pants when we land. Don't worry; I'll take good care of you. Later, you'll tell your friends how much you enjoyed the flight."

Ty thought about grown men throwing up and peeing their pants, and he started to smile. He wasn't going to do any of those things. He looked at Mike with admiration as he started to understand his sinister humor. He even thought maybe he'd like to become a bush pilot, so he could make someone pee their pants. Ty felt a lot better now. He and Joseph looked at each other and began to laugh. It was a nervous sounding laugh, but they started having fun anyway.

The plane touched down like it was settling onto pillows. Spray washed over Joseph and Ty's windows. The lake looked five times the size of a football field, one third of it still covered with ice. Mike turned the plane away from the ice and taxied slowly toward a grassy bank that bordered a lush green spring meadow.

As the plane drew closer to the bank, Mike cut the engine. Zane got out onto the pontoon, clipped one end of a rope to the plane and then leapt to the shore.

"Time to get out, boys," Mike said.

Joseph and Ty were charged with excitement. Joseph grabbed the black duffel, and Ty took the day pack. Mike helped them out and onto the bank.

"Okay, boys," Zane said, "take off those pants and shoes and put these on." Zane tossed them their boots, pants, and breechclouts. Zane pulled three purse-sized bags with shoulder straps out of the duffel. One was about half as big as the other two. Ty's bag had a raining cloud burned into the leather flap that closed it. Joseph's bag displayed a coyote looking out of its den. Zane's had a sitting black bear.

Zane divided what had been the contents of the boy's pockets into Joseph's and Ty's bags. He put on his pants, boots, breechclout, and leather shirt. Zane then collected all the clothes and the day pack, shoving them into the duffel.

While Joseph and Ty admired their new leather clothes and examined the contents of their bags, Zane took the duffel over to Mike.

"Will you put this into the truck for me?"

"Sure. You know it gets cold up here?" Mike said, obviously concerned.

"We'll be fine. Call my wife for me when you can, and tell her that we got in okay, will you? And thanks for everything. And, Mike, don't fly over. We came up here to get away from traffic."

Mike smiled and shook Zane's hand. "Good hunting," he said as he pushed off from the bank and hopped onto the pontoon. A minute later, Mike was taxiing out into the main body of the lake.

Zane and the boys watched Mike circle once, tip his wings and head northeast to meet Lisa seventy miles away. Then silence filled the crisp air. If it hadn't been for Joseph and Ty's polar fleece jackets, Zane and the boys would have looked like a part of the landscape of two hundred years ago.

As the plane disappeared into the horizon, the reality of the task ahead finally settled in. The boys started to feel excited, nervous, hungry, and cold all at one time.

They were on the eastern slope of the North Cascades at about 6,500-foot elevation. Snow covered mountains rose straight from the edge of the lake to the west. Patches of snow crowded the trees all around. It would be a cold night.

"All right, Joseph," Zane said. "What's first?"

"Shelter," Joseph said proudly.

"That's right, always: shelter, water, food. This area is clear of snow, mostly because of the sun but partly because of the wind. So, let's move a little ways into the trees." Zane started across the meadow toward the trees. "Guys, we're going to build a small wickiup. We want to find a spot fifty to a hundred yards from the edge of the trees. Stay together but move fast. I'll meet you back here in about half an hour."

"Okay, Dad. Let's go, Ty," Joseph said, taking command.

Trotting through the trees, the boys breathed in their love for the earth and bounded along with a youthful confidence that together they could survive anything.

Joseph and Ty glided through the flora.

What a beautiful place, Ty thought. *I could live here forever.*

As Ty ran, his boots felt warm and snug on his feet. He was light and fast, like a deer bounding through the forest.

Joseph knew Ty relied on him when they were together. He didn't mind. He liked being in charge. He enjoyed helping and leading. Joseph knew Ty would fool around, coasting beside him. But Ty was the toughest kid he knew. And Joseph knew he could count on him if things ever turned bad.

"Ty, let's check this out," Joseph said, running toward a large granite boulder.

The boys vaulted small logs and ran between trees, resembling warriors in pursuit of a fleeing enemy.

"This place is perfect," Ty yelled as the boys reached the small rock outcropping.

Joseph looked around, carefully taking in the strengths and weaknesses of the potential camp so that he could answer their father's questions.

"Let's get Dad," Joseph said.

Ty nodded. "Let's go." Then he took off as fast as he could go.

Joseph ran after him, yelling, "Ty, wait up!"

Ty stopped and looked back. It took a moment for him to find Joseph among the trees. "What's wrong?" Ty asked.

"Wait up." Joseph trotted up to his brother. "Ty, you better slow down. You're going too fast, and you're not paying attention. You're going to get us lost if you keep running off without thinking like that."

"I was just going to get Dad." A slight shiver of fear passed through him as he processed the thought of being lost. What would happen if he was lost out here in the snow, in the mountains with no matches, all alone? The cold damp breeze sent a shiver down Ty's back as he looked around and realized he wasn't sure which way his father had gone. He wasn't even positive which way the lake was. The desolate empty feeling that feeds the cancer of fear moved from his stomach up into his chest. "Maybe you should lead."

"Let's get Dad. That's a great camp spot, isn't it?" Joseph

asked as he led the way in a different direction than Ty had been running.

Zane saw his boys coming toward him. He had not found any viable camp areas in his direction. The ground had been gently sloping down. With the snow melt, the ground had gotten wetter the farther he walked. Wending his way around large melting snow patches, he found little more than wet boggy ground. He felt like he was walking into a cold pocket. The boys' grinning faces showed that they had had better luck.

"Dad, we found the perfect place!" Joseph shouted.

"Yeah," Ty agreed. "It has a dead tree with bark for a shelter and everything."

Joseph looked at Ty, a little surprised. He hadn't thought that Ty had really evaluated the camp area's natural resources.

Ty looked back with his mischievous prideful smile.

"Well, let's take a look," Zane said.

Joseph and Ty lead the way as the three leather clad males loped gracefully through the forest.

Joseph had to double back a short way to find the rock outcropping again. As they walked into the small open area, Joseph and Ty were even more proud of their discovery.

Zane surveyed the area. The ground was firm, and there was good cover from the wind. It appeared that there was easy access to firewood and resources for building a shelter, and they were close to the lake for fresh water. There was even a rock outcropping that would gather the warmth from the fire and aid in the overall comfort of the camp. "This is the place, boys."

SEVEN

Timber circled an area about fifty to sixty feet across. From where they stood, a large boulder on their right took up one third of the open area and stood ten feet at its highest point. Extending from there to the opposite side was a tumble of large to small rocks. To their left were the remains of a large Douglas fir that had been struck by lightning. The once towering, majestic tree was now a fractured sixty-foot-high trunk circled by slabs of fallen bark. What had been the top half now lay from the base of the tree, extending across the rock pile into the far side of the clearing. In front of them was an area twenty-five-feet by fifteen-feet, covered with clumps of grass and small bushes.

"Boys, we have two hours," Zane said. "Gather boughs, about three feet in length. Pile them right there. Don't get big thick branches. Cut nothing bigger than one inch thick."

"All right, Dad," Ty said, drawing his knife.

"You got it, Dad," Joseph agreed, pulling out his knife.

The boys headed off in different directions.

Zane went to the great tree and kicked five brittle branches off the fallen top. After clearing an area from the base of the large boulder into the rock and boulder pile of all movable rocks, Zane broke his branches into seven- to eight-foot lengths. He then wedged the thicker ends into the base of the rock pile, boulder and around in a circle. The tapered part of the branches braced together at the top, making a frame about eight feet across and four and one-half feet high in the center. It looked like the frame of a short tepee that was tucked close to the large boulder of the out-cropping.

The boys worked hard, and when Zane had the frame completed, they added another load of branches to the impressive pile of boughs.

"Is this good enough?" Ty asked.

"The more you get, the warmer we'll be," Zane said. "I'd get as much as you have time for. Don't move too far from here, though. It's easy to lose your way out here."

Zane left the boys to their labors and went off to see what he could do about something to eat. The crisp fresh air filled his lungs, and the sweet smell of the rich damp earth sharpened his senses. Moving into the trees, Zane stayed low and quietly slipped from cover to cover as he scanned the forest for movement. This was the most productive time, this last hour of the day. As he moved along, he paid close attention to downed trees and brushy areas. He looked for game trails and edible plants. As he hunted, Zane picked up a stick about two feet long and half as thick as his wrist.

Stealthily, almost crawling from bush to tree, he scanned for movement or a distinctive shape, a pair of eyes, a curve of a back—anything that would give away something that could feed his young sons. Zane watched and listened.

Three pine squirrels playfully foraged in a tangle of downed trees. Zane crept up to the edge of the logs, then settled in with his back against a tree where two fallen trees crossed. The squirrels saw him move in and scooted away to safety. Zane raised his arm up next to the tree behind him, cocked the stick back and waited.

Five minutes passed and a mosquito landed on Zane's face, ate his fill, and moved on. Five minutes passed. Three more mosquitoes were attached to his face and ear. Zane's left ankle was asleep.

His right shoulder had ached from the strain of holding his arm vertical for a while, but he relaxed his mind to the discomfort. A squirrel poked its head up a couple of times, curious but cautious. Finally, it couldn't stand the tension of the wait and skittered down the tree, barking and screaming at what was laying in the middle of his area.

The bold little squirrel charged and retreated, getting more and more aggressive until it dodged past Zane. He swung the stick sharply across the log and struck the squirrel square across the back. Zane set up a deadfall trap, baiting it with a bit of the squirrel's intestine. Zane then made a quick loop to the meadow, picked some wild onions and edible water plants. He looked up at the mountains. This is where he felt alive, where his heart told him that his spirit belonged. He breathed deeply of the cool spring air, scanned the meadow and then hurried back to camp.

Joseph and Ty had built wickiups on past trips. They knew what to do. It was like laying shingles on a roof to shed the rain. They started by placing the branches completely around the bottom of the frame, then overlapping that layer they positioned another course of branches up higher and continued that way up and over the top. Then, they repeated at the bottom a second time and applied another thickness of branches the same as the first. With the wickiup covered over, they layered additional fir boughs about six inches thick on the floor of their new home.

Joseph and Ty had been working as fast as they could for an hour and a half. Sweating and tired, they tucked the last fir boughs into place and collapsed onto their forest mattress. It wasn't as nice as a feather bed, but it was shelter from the cold.

"Great job, boys," Zane said as he walked into camp. "All we need now is the bark. Do you guys want to gather and place the bark, or make a fire ring and cook this squirrel?"

Joseph and Ty's heads rose. They hadn't thought about how hungry they were.

"I'm starving," said Ty.

"Yeah, me, too," said Joseph. "We'll do the cooking, okay, Ty?"

"Sounds good to me," agreed Ty.

"Okay then, fire ring here," Zane said, drawing an X in the dirt with a stick. "And pile the firewood here."

Ty's shoulders slumped. He didn't know that cooking meant firewood, fire ring, and everything.

"You will appreciate being tired tonight when it's cold and you're trying to sleep. We'd better hurry, it's getting dark." Zane said.

Zane went to the base of the old pine tree and collected several large slabs of bark. He arranged them around the wickiup in overlapping courses to the top, the same as the boys had done with the branches. He saved a large piece to use as a door, to cover the two-foot-wide by three-foot-high opening the boys had left for an entrance. The branches that the boys had placed acted as insulation, and the bark formed the little shelter's watertight roof.

Joseph and Ty had prepared the fire with a small tinder nest below a tripod of small to larger sticks. To the side there was a supply of feeder sticks ready to stoke a blaze as it developed.

Joseph looked up at his father. "Dad, could you start this for us?"

Ty looked tired and cold. He knew Joseph could start it, but it might take him a long time.

Zane reached into his leather bag and pulled out three wooden matches. "Fire lessons start tomorrow," Zane said as he handed Joseph the matches. "I have a trap to check. I'll be right back."

Joseph held the matches in front of him. They were like jewels. For a moment, the boys looked at them like a wish had been granted.

Joseph very carefully fluffed the tinder. Ty readied different sizes of dry branches to feed the fire. Joseph carefully struck the match and a moment later hot crackling flames licked up through the layers of sticks.

"We did it," Ty said, looking at the remaining matches.

"Yeah," Joseph said. "You better keep these." He handed Ty the two remaining matches.

Ty accepted them like they were the gift of life and carefully tucked them into a safe dry place within his bag.

Zane approached the tangle of logs where he had gotten the squirrel. The sun had been down for a while. The last rays of waning light were receding quickly through the timber, leaving a soft violet glow radiating from the other side of the snow-covered ridges.

The dead fall had been tripped. That didn't always mean food, but it was a good sign. Zane raised his stick and peered over the leg-sized log that was the weight of the trap. A squirrel bounded off. Zane swung at it, but the squirrel was too fast. The stick swished past the squirrel's tail as it dove into a hole that led beneath the pile of logs.

Zane looked back to his trap. A dead squirrel was half pinned beneath it. The other squirrel had been paying his last respects to his fallen friend.

This was a good sign. Two small squirrels and a few handfuls of greens weren't a lot, but it was a long way from going hungry. It didn't always go this well.

Zane didn't reset his trap. Two squirrels from one place were enough. Never take too much, Zane thought as he moved quickly back toward camp.

Zane and the boys carefully skinned the squirrels, saving the guts for bait, and the brains for tanning the skins.

The boys were experienced woodsmen to a point. The chores of hunting camp were familiar to them, but they always learned new skills and improved on previous lessons. This was their first trip with no extra clothing, sleeping, or hunting equipment and no larder of food. The difference was striking, the danger of the task chillingly real.

"A squirrel's skin doesn't amount to much," Zane said, "but on a survival trip you save everything. We can use these skins for making weapons, carrying bait, making traps, and so on. When you start from nothing, everything has value."

While the boys cooked the squirrels skewered flat onto roasting sticks, Zane built a wall of stones. The wall started next to the fire ring and extended out from the boulder. It was about three feet in height and five feet long. With a small fire, the heat reflected from the wall and boulder, radiating a gentle warmth over Zane and the boys' backs and shoulders.

"This is the best camping trip I've ever been on," Ty said, finishing his meager dinner.

"I don't know," Joseph said, smiling. "I think I'd rather be in school doing algebra."

Zane, Joseph, and Ty all looked at each other, then laughed until they were rolling on the ground.

That night in the wickiup, Joseph lay against the far wall, Ty in the middle, and Zane in last next to the door. Then Zane covered them all deep in pine boughs. They slept the sleep of tired men. They dreamed the dreams of warriors.

As Zane's eyes opened, the forest smell filled his senses. Pitch from the boughs stuck to his hair and his hands. He sat up slowly in the crowded room.

"Dad, are you getting up?" Joseph asked.

"Yes. Do you want to come?"

"Yeah," Joseph said, reaching around in the blackness of the wickiup for his bag, trying not to wake Ty.

Zane and Joseph slipped out through the small opening into the frigid night air. Joseph's chin dropped down into his jacket as the light breeze pushed painfully into any exposed skin. He hadn't realized how cold it was outside their tiny pine house.

"What time is it?" Joseph asked.

"It should be light in a couple of hours," Zane said looking around.

"Dad, I had the weirdest dream last night." He turned his collar up and dug his hands deep into his pockets.

"Think about it as we walk. When it's not so cold, we'll sit down, and you can tell it to me." Zane reached under the edge of the wickiup and took out the squirrel skins. He wrapped the trap bait into one and put both into his pouch.

"We're going to take a walk and set some traps. It's easy to forget where your traps are when you set them in the dark, so pay extra attention," Zane said as they moved off into the trees.

Joseph tried to move quietly. He felt cold and stiff, but as long as he was moving it was bearable. The half moon produced more shadow than light. Branches jabbed his legs as he groped and guessed his way through the thick forest. He was thankful for his warm feet and the protection of his leather pants and breech clout.

After a few minutes, Joseph's eyes became comfortable with the dark world that surrounded him. He learned that once he stopped fighting the cold, it wasn't as bad. Once he started to look beyond the branches and trees next to him, he traveled through the tangle instead of fighting for every stride.

The light opened up the world around them as the two hunters came to the edge of a meadow. Zane crouched low with Joseph following. They carefully approached the clearing, staying no higher than the top of the brush.

The star-filled sky lit the meadow with an opaque clarity. High mountain brush interspersed with clumps of grass extended to a small creek no more than six feet wide that flowed to the lake that they had landed in the night before. The meadow continued off to the right about one hundred and fifty yards to where the forest had boxed it in. To the left, the meadow expanded beyond the limits of their vision. The area was dotted with patches of trees, like tall black islands in the pre-morning dawn.

On the other side of the creek, snowy ridges covered with

timber led to a higher country that was frozen over and looked ominously cold. It was a place that Joseph had no desire to explore.

As Zane and Joseph watched the meadow, two large bull elk trotted out from the canyon almost directly across from them. Their magnificent antlers had dropped during the early spring, but they had the beginnings of what would be this year's racks extending above their ears. Laying their heads back as they trotted briskly across the meadow, they had the posture of bulls accustomed to carrying weight on their heads. The two proud old ghosts of the woods crossed the meadow quickly and disappeared into the trees to Zane and Joseph's left.

Joseph wasn't cold any longer. He wondered how his dad intended to ambush these elk.

Zane looked at his son and answered his unasked question. "Those were wise old men, Joseph," Zane said. "We won't be taking them home this trip."

Zane took out a squirrel skin, laid it on a dead branch, and cut it into several long strips. He returned the tail to his pouch. Three of the strips he tied to sticks that he had prepared the night before. The remaining strips he connected into a strip about one and a half feet long.

Joseph had learned a long time ago that patience was the greatest lesson. He did not ask a question if he thought the answer would become evident without words. He watched and he listened. His father was a good teacher who, for the most part, offered a clear picture as he unfolded life's lessons.

Halfway across the meadow, Zane set a rabbit snare with the long strip. It was a loop snare with a light spring. He bent down a small branch of a bush for the spring, careful not to make it so strong that it would break the delicate strap.

Moving west to one of the clumps of trees, they set a Paiute deadfall. This was Zane's favorite small game trap. The stick trigger was held together by a small strap, making it easy to carry and set up. Many years of practice allowed Zane to set them with deadly efficiency.

They quickly set and baited a series of small traps, as they made their way down the creek to the lake.

From atop the granite boulders that formed the south-west border of the lake, Zane and Joseph gazed out into the crystalline water. In the morning calm, small fish hunted the shallows, rising for small emergers or terrestrials that fell onto the glass like surface. Looking down into the transparent depths, life was shrouded with shadow and reflection.

"This place has changed very little through the generations," Zane said. "Our ancestors stood on this very spot and enjoyed sunrises like this one. Maybe those two wise old men we saw this morning were telling us welcome home. Let's take a bath. Then you can tell me about your vision."

A chill ran up Joseph's back. He had been afraid that his dream last night was more than a dream. It had been too real. Had he seen his father's death?

"If you wait until it warms up, you will have to grow roots," Zane joked.

Realizing his father was already half undressed, he pulled his clothes off as fast as he could and charged into the frigid water. The cold hit him like a wall.

"Cold, isn't it?" Zane said with a smile, wading in after him.

"I think I'm standing in a hot spring. It's toasty over here." Joseph tried to say it with a straight face, but his teeth were chattering, and goose bumps covered his body.

Zane and Joseph both laughed then screamed with exhilaration. They splashed each other a few times then light footed it for the shore. The rocks weren't warm enough to lay on yet, so they stood shivering in the sun and stripped the water off themselves with their hands. Then they quickly pulled their leather clothes over their damp skin. Joseph followed his father's lead and rubbed his tingling legs to get the circulation going.

EIGHT

"Okay, tell me your dream."

"Dad," Joseph began, "what is the difference between a dream and a vision?"

Zane thought for a while, and then he answered. "You could find opposing answers to that question in every culture. But this is something I know. Sometimes the spirit world speaks to us through our dreams. When this happens, it is not a dream, it is a vision.

"I've never known it to happen in the city. The spirits of our ancestors don't live there. They speak to us here when we walk amongst them, and when we open our hearts to their wisdom. When we come up to these places, we honor them by remembering their ways. If you had a vision last night, it could be their way of honoring you."

"Well, it started like this." Joseph recounted his dream, lost in its memory, as if interpreting a story watched on a screen. "I was standing in a thick fog. You were lying on the ground. This is the part that scares me. Your head was wrapped in bandages and your face was covered in blood. I was covering you over with leaves and branches."

Joseph paused and thought for a moment, wanting to

remember every detail. "By your feet sat an old black bear. I could tell he was old, because he had a lot of gray hair on his muzzle and head. The bear said, 'Thank you, my cousin.' I smiled at him. Then everything just drifted away. Do you know what it means?" He didn't press his father for a quick answer. The telling of his dream had weakened him. His knees shook, but he didn't feel cold.

"When I was thirteen, my grandfather took me on a trip," Zane said. "On that trip I had a vision. My grandfather never told me what it meant. I'll tell it to you now."

"I was walking in a cloud. I was walking like my grandfather walked, quietly with leather clothes. A black bear walked up to me. He was a huge coal black bear. He was fierce and powerful, so I was afraid. He sat down in front of me, so I sat down, too. We sat there looking at each other for a long time before the bear spoke. 'Who are you, little man?' he asked. I said, 'I am a Nez Perce warrior.' He looked at me for a long time again and said, 'When you are truly a warrior, bring me a war lance.' Then the bear got up, walked away from me and disappeared into the mist.

"My grandfather wouldn't interpret my vision. He said that I was too young and that when I was ready, it would interpret itself. But that is how I came to be known as Sitting Bear. I can tell you this, Joseph," Zane said. "The spirit in your vision means you no harm. And I don't think the bear of your vision will kill me, either. Let's get back to camp." Zane stood up and warmed his face toward the rising sun. "Ty should be up by now."

Zane and Joseph walked back to their camp. They found Ty still in the wickiup.

He rolled over and smiled. "Is it warm yet? Where have you guys been?"

"It's time to get up, son. You and Joseph have traps to check."

"Got it covered," Joseph responded.

"You guys have fun. I'll see you this evening," Zane said.

That is exactly what Ty and Joseph wanted to hear. This was a day to explore.

Ty abandoned his pine bed, and the two boys trotted off. Free for the day, they opened their hearts and minds, and allowed the smells, the sights, and the sounds to propel them into their adventure.

After a short while, they approached the place where Zane and Joseph had set the traps. The boys crept slowly to the edge of the meadow. Forty yards in front of them, a rabbit was frantically trying to run away from the snare that held it firmly to the small bush.

Ty started to set out after it, but Joseph grabbed his pant leg and pulled him back. Then Ty saw two very large dogs trotting swiftly toward the panicked rabbit.

"Wolves," Ty said. He sat back down with his mouth open, his hair felt like it was standing straight up. One of the young wolves turned and snarled at its companion. A moment later the two massive dogs growled and tore at each other, fighting for the right to eat the terrified rabbit that had retreated into the brush as far as the tether would allow. After a couple of moments of vicious sparring, the smaller of the two gave way to the other. The victor ripped the rabbit free from the snare and ran off to consume his prize.

When the wolves had gone, the boys ventured out into the clearing, freshly aware of the conscienceless reality of the world outside of the laws of man.

The boys worked their way along the trap line, checking and resetting. They found another rabbit and a small squirrel. After they moved and reset the last trap, they sat down to roast their breakfast.

Joseph carefully selected the tinder and arranged it into a little nest. He then took out a piece of flint from his bag and struck it with the back of his knife. After ten minutes of trying, he caught a spark, blew it into life, and built a fire. Ty roasted the rabbit while Joseph prepared the squirrel.

"Joseph, those wolves were awesome, weren't they?"

"Yeah, they sure were."

"You don't think they'd come after us, do you?" Ty asked.

"I don't think so, but you never know," Joseph said. "Should we make some spears?"

The wolves had shaken Ty up. His dad was always at home in the forest. It was like he belonged here, as did the wolves. Ty knew he belonged out here, too, but sometimes he felt more like the rabbit, dangling from a bush, hoping that nothing with big teeth would find him.

Joseph was different from Ty, and Ty knew it. When they were in remote places, something changed in Joseph. He seemed to see things. He intuitively knew what to do. Ty knew that the wolves had affected Joseph, too. But it was different. Joseph didn't fear them.

When the boys finished their meal, they went to a nearby willow stand and cut staves. They sharpened one end to a long sharp point. Effective for an animal with soft skin. It was better than nothing.

They practiced throwing their new weapons at whatever looked like a good target. The spear felt good in Ty's hand. He tried three throws at a rabbit size bush, about twenty feet away and hit it twice. Ty was a natural with any weapon. When he threw or shot at something, he expected to hit it, and most times he did. He couldn't outshoot his dad yet, but Ty felt that it was only a matter of time.

"I want to check out a canyon about a quarter mile back up the creek," Joseph said. "This morning Dad and I saw two elk come out of it."

"Elk! You didn't tell me you saw elk! Were they big? Did they have antlers?"

"They were both bulls. They were growing this year's racks, but they weren't that big yet. You need to keep your voice down, Ty. If you talk so loud, we may as well go back to camp, because you'll scare everything within a mile, and we won't be seeing anything."

Ty didn't say anything. He didn't like Joseph talking to him that way, but he knew he had been loud. A couple of times they had seen ground squirrels run off. Now that he had a weapon, he wanted to get close enough for a throw. Traps can feed you, but this was honest hunting. Ty was the wolf now, and it made him feel good. Ty wouldn't make that mistake again.

The boys worked their way back up toward the canyon. Once Ty took a long throw, but his target was gone before the spear hit the ground.

"Man, there's a lot of game here," Ty said.

"I bet these animals have never seen people," Joseph said. "I don't think it was a terribly hard winter, either. I bet this year, our lake doesn't clear off until the end of June."

"If I get a throw at an elk, should I take it?" Ty asked.

Joseph looked at him and thought for a moment before speaking. "We had better not. We are not going to go hungry here, and Dad could get into big trouble if we got caught by Fish and Game. Besides, our spears aren't heavy or sharp enough to get an elk."

Ty looked at his spear and hefted it, smiled, and continued down the trail.

Joseph and Ty reached the mouth of the deep canyon that skirted the snow-covered ridge.

"You lead the way," Joseph said. "You are better with your spear than I am. If we see something, you'd have a better chance."

Ty puffed with pride and led the way up the heavily traveled trail.

"This place is a freeway," Ty whispered. "Elk, deer, coyotes, bears, wolves, everything uses this trail."

Joseph grinned with excitement.

The two boys smiled at each other, bumped fists and continued up the path.

Moving quietly down the path, they made slow but steady progress. At one point a small doe crossed the trail ahead of them. Joseph and Ty didn't even know if it had seen them, but it was too far away to pursue. They were looking for small game, anyway.

After a couple of hours, they stepped out of the thick timber into a small valley with an open meadow. The boys looked for any movement in the grass. They weren't going to set any traps this far out. This was strictly fair chase hunting.

The new valley had patches of trees and small meadows like the one they were camped in. There was also a more westerly exposure, which meant more moisture. The boys picked their way around the snowbanks, crossing the icy mounds only when there was no other option. They decided to turn south for a while and then circle the valley.

Another half hour of hard hiking, the distance to camp, along with the increasing cold and dampness of their boots and clothing, became a concern to both Ty and Joseph. The young explorers turned back toward the base of the cold dark ridge, hoping to be back at camp well before nightfall.

The generally level to rolling terrain with large areas of tall timber became disorienting for Joseph. He decided to cut across a small meadow. Halfway across, he spotted fresh moccasin tracks in the soft earth. He looked around in disbelief and showed them to Ty.

The reality that somehow, they had walked in a circle sent a sick panic through Ty's core. After a couple of minutes, they discussed which way to go. Ty had an opinion but was happy to let Joseph make the decision.

"The mouth of the canyon is over there," Joseph said, pointing to the farthest point of the half circle of ridge line. "Let's head straight across."

"Sounds good to me," Ty said. He had no desire to navigate.

Moving at a swift pace toward their landmark, the boys passed through several small meadow openings. As they neared the place where they expected to turn to the trail that would lead them to camp, they stepped up to another large clearing. Approaching from the south side, the boys crossed a shallow but wide patch of snow. The snowfield covered most of the clearing. Joseph and Ty scanned the area for anything moving and then moved out onto the frozen drift of hard packed snow.

Joseph was stepping off the icy bank of snow when Ty yelled from behind him.

"Joseph! Check this out!"

About twenty feet behind him, Ty stood next to a bush that Joseph had walked past. Laying half in the bush and half under the snow was a frozen spike elk.

Joseph ran back and stood next to Ty.

"I can't believe I didn't see it."

"If it had been alive, it would have bitten you," Ty said with a laugh in his voice. "What do you think we should do with it?"

"Frozen in like this, he's not going anywhere. We don't have a lot of time, anyway. Let's get back and tell Dad."

Joseph and Ty's minds raced. This elk was like finding a country store. Everything they needed to make life comfortable was there frozen into the snow.

They moved fast now. The sun was approaching the western ridge line. Their feet and hands cold, both experienced a growing feeling of something less friendly about this new valley.

Ty glanced behind him to make sure they weren't being followed.

I'm glad I wasn't here with you last winter, cousin, Joseph thought as he recalled the frozen elk's lifeless eyes.

The boys moved fast and soon reached the meadow where they had seen the wolves.

"We better collect our traps," Joseph said.

"Shouldn't we do that tomorrow?"

"This place has been good to us. We don't want to take too much," Joseph said with authority.

"Okay, but I'd leave them another night."

· · ·

The boys spread out and collected the traps. They had gotten a chipmunk and a beautiful black and white weasel. Added to the squirrel they had from earlier, it was enough, but not a lot for the three of them.

As the boys jogged the last half mile back to camp, they reflected on their day. They had seen things today that most grown men would never see. They had gone places where most boys their age would have gotten lost and possibly died of exposure.

Even just today makes this the best trip I've ever been on, Ty thought. He couldn't wait to tell Dad about the elk and the wolves.

NINE

Joseph sometimes wondered if he had lived too long in town to really fit in out here. But he felt most at home in wild country. He didn't know if he possessed the fierceness of his ancestors; if he truly had their will to survive. He kept thinking back to the young elk's eyes, which contained no resolve to live in them. It was as if he had laid down to rest and the cold overtook him. Joseph knew that wouldn't happen to Ty. Ty had always been a fighter. Death would take him screaming and striking. And Dad . . . Dad wouldn't go until he was ready. Then he would embrace it and soar with the eagles. Joseph hoped death wouldn't simply overtake him. When his day came, he wanted to die with honor.

Zane watched his sons until they trotted out of sight. *I'm a lucky man to have two wonderful sons,* Zane thought. *My father died when I was two years old. I wonder if he sees his grandsons when I bring them here. Thank you, Great Spirit, for sending my grandfather to teach me the old ways.*

For Zane this day was one of fasting and prayer. He walked in the opposite direction from his sons. He went past the cold canyon he had seen the evening before. Soon he came to a wide, gently down-sloping valley. The meadow meandered along with the stream that poured out from the bottom of the lake. It was a beautiful patchwork of trees amongst the green grass and wildflowers. The picture was framed by high timber, extending up to the ridge lines on all sides.

The presence of God filled Zane with awe and wonder. A sense of peace and thankfulness welled up inside of him. He sat down, looking with reverence out onto the sunbaked valley. Alive in all of spring's finery, the valley displayed life with a new clarity.

Like a blind man who could now see, Zane visioned deer, coyote, squirrels, rabbits, and all types of birds as they crossed or fed in the valley. He saw the bees in the flowers and the branches of the trees bending in the gentle breeze. Zane lifted his hands up toward the sky and gave thanks. He offered a gift of smoke from his pipe to the east, south, west and north.

It's good to be alive, Zane thought. *Thank you, Hunyawat, for making me a Nez Perce.*

Bolting from the trees, Zane ran out into the valley, like a rabbit whose life hangs on the outcome of each race. He ran for an hour, finally stopping at a creek that poured out of the mountains with the spring snow melt.

Zane built a small sweat lodge next to a deep pool. The sweat lodge was similar in design yet smaller and more Spartan than the wickiup he and the boys had built the night before. Then he built a fire to heat rocks to heat the lodge. After cleansing himself with sage and cedar, he used sticks to carry the hot rocks into the center of the lodge, then slowly poured water over them. The steam hissed and rolled off the rocks, filling the tiny room. The damp heat burned his nostrils, cleansed his spirit, and purified his body.

Zane spent the rest of the day until nightfall, sweating, praying, and giving thanks for his wife, his sons, and the world that fed his spirit and body. After four rounds of prayer, songs, and plunging into the icy pool, Zane was physically and emotionally spent.

. . .

Joseph and Ty arrived back at camp, disappointed and missing their father. Feeling comfort in each other's presence, the two boys settled into the chores of camp.

Ty gathered the firewood. Joseph started to prepare the evening meal. He first skinned the musky smelling weasel, being careful around the ears, eyes, and lips. Ty gathered the tinder from the sagebrush in the meadow and made a little nest. He took a piece of flint out of his pouch and struck the edge of it downward with the back of his knife. A spark flew off.

Ty tried again and again until finally a good spark landed into the nest of tinder. Ty blew with hope and anticipation. He blew like he was telling a secret to the spark that would bring it to life. Then the spark heard him and sprang into a flame. Ty's heart leapt; he quickly fed the burning nest while fire licked up toward his grinning face.

"Got the fire going," Ty said, trying to sound as casual as he could.

"Good job, Ty. Why don't you build it up then bank it with some rocks? Then we can go out to the lake and get a drink."

"Okay, I could drink the whole lake."

Ty added small, then larger sticks to his fire, then piled rocks over it. *This looks safe,* he thought. "Let's get going."

The boys picked up their spears and took off. Ty caught Joseph's casual look at the fire as they walked out of camp.

Shadows stretched out from the trees that waved to the gentle breeze. The smell of spring carried a rush of fresh memories to Ty's senses. Squirrels chattered and raced through the branches one last time before turning in for the night. Birds sang to each other and to anyone else that would care to listen. A stellar jay flew over and landed in a tree above the boys. Calling and calling, the jay let everyone know that there were visitors amongst them.

Joseph and Ty took off their boots, pulled up their pants, and dangled their tired feet in the crystal cold water.

"Joe," Ty said, "where do you think Dad is?

"I don't know. I've been wondering, too. He would have told us if he were going to be out overnight, though."

"What if he got hurt? What should we do if he doesn't come back?"

"Well, I guess we'd wait until tomorrow, then see if we could find him," Joseph said.

Joseph felt sure that their father was okay, but it never hurt to go over possibilities. It was even fun. Joseph and Ty used to make a game of it. What if . . . then what would we do? Sometimes it would go on for hours. Joseph kind of missed the game sometimes. Ty would try to lead him into it still, but Joseph wouldn't let it go on and on anymore. Life was changing for Joseph. There was too much on his mind to fill it up with that kind of fantasy.

"I'm really hungry," Ty said. "All I've had to eat today is half of that rabbit, some wild onions, and that Miners lettuce we got from the creek."

"I'm hungry, too. Let's pick anything we can find to eat on the way back. We'll have a feast," Joseph said with a smile.

"All right!" Ty agreed.

The boys put on their boots and forged their way back toward camp, arriving as the light faded into the west. They carefully laid the plants harvested on a large flat rock, keeping each kind separate. They had collected two good mushrooms, a handful of Miners lettuce, and a couple of wild onions.

The boys roasted the squirrel, chipmunk, and the weasel. Then they ate the squirrel and all the vegetables they wanted.

Joseph and Ty were as tired as they had ever been, but they felt a warm contentment. It had been an extraordinary day. They had seen wolves. They had found the frozen elk. They had harvested food from the wild, and now they sat in front of a warm fire, listening to the night sounds and reflecting on the day with full stomachs.

"Joseph," Ty said with a smile, "we did it, we survived."

"Yeah, we sure did." Joseph smiled back.

The two boys reached over in a high-five.

"Dad's going to be excited to know there are wolves around," Ty said.

"That was really something, wasn't it?" Joseph replied. "I'm glad I wasn't that rabbit."

"Me, too."

TEN

Zane felt renewed in the spirit, closer to the earth. When he stepped out of the sweat lodge the final time, the richness of life engulfed him. He was beyond the trappings of man; he now stood in the real world again. Leaving the lodge, he walked briskly back to camp in the semi-darkness of the moonlit sky.

The coals were still hot from the boy's evening fire when Zane entered the camp clearing. He knelt to stir the red embers with a roasting stick. As he warmed his cold hands, a shiver ran down his back. It's cold.

If I had a coat, I'd put it on, Zane thought as he smiled. *We'll have to see what we can do about that.*

Zane slipped through the small entrance into the wickiup and then replaced the door. The boys had added some extra branches from the inside against the opening for additional insulation.

Good idea, Zane thought as he replaced the boughs.

"Is that you, Dad?" Joseph asked.

"Yeah, how was your day?" Zane replied, feeling his way into the darkness.

"It was great!"

"It was the best!" Ty added.

"How about you?" Joseph asked.

"I had a good day. I built a sweat lodge. In a few days, maybe we can all go and use it together."

"That sounds great!" Ty said, sounding less tired. "We saw some wolves and a frozen elk."

"You were lucky. You don't see wolves very often. Tell me everything in the morning, okay."

"Good night, Dad," Joseph said.

"Good night, Dad. I love you," Ty added.

"I love you, too, son. I'm really proud of what you guys did today." Zane settled into a comfortable position and immediately fell into a deep sleep.

Zane's eyes snapped open, instinctively reaching for his knife. Something was moving on the other side of the thin wall of the wickiup. He strained his ears, trying to determine what was there. They sounded too small for a bear and too fast for a raccoon. It was coyotes or wolves, two or three of them. If it was coyotes, he would set a trap.

Time to get up, anyway, Zane thought, reaching for his boots.

The night hunters moved off a little way, watched for a few minutes, and then slipped away into the timber. They were looking for a more substantial meal than a few bones dropped around a fire anyway.

Zane laced up his boots and put his leather bag around his neck. "Let's get moving, guys," he said gently, shaking Ty's shoulder.

"Okay, I'm up," Ty said in his sleep.

Joseph felt his way in the dark of the wickiup till he found a place where he could sit up. Then he checked his knife and started to search for his leather bag.

"Come on, Ty, time to get up," Zane repeated, shaking Ty again.

"Okay, I'm up," Ty said, rubbing his eyes and looking around. "It sure is dark in here."

"Let's get going. We have some traps to set," Zane said, clearing away the boughs next to the door.

"Did you eat your dinner last night, Dad? We cooked some food for you. We hung it inside the door," Joseph said. "I forgot to tell you last night."

"That's okay. You guys eat it. You have to keep your strength up."

"We can share them," Ty said.

"No, you go ahead. I'll eat soon enough."

Knowing their father was ready to go, Joseph and Ty devoured the food as quickly as they could.

"Give me all the bones, guys," Zane said, holding one hand against each of his sons so they could find it in the dark.

Zane took the bones outside and set them on a rock, then placed other rocks over them. He would use them later to bait a trap.

Joseph and Ty got out into the night air, stretching, and rubbing the sleep out of their eyes.

"What time is it?" Ty asked, looking into the night sky.

"It should be light in a couple of hours," Joseph answered, smiling at his father.

Zane led the boys out of camp in the same direction that he had gone the previous morning.

He carried his throwing stick in a long pocket sewn into the back of his shirt. The boys carried their spears.

I'm glad we picked up the traps yesterday, Joseph thought as he followed his father through the dark trees.

Ty had a hard time keeping up at first. When Joseph backed

off, and Ty walked in between Zane and Joseph, it went a lot better.

An hour before light, Zane and his sons arrived at the valley that he had watched the previous morning. The three hunters crept up to the edge of the trees and looked out onto the star lit meadow.

"Joseph, did you pick up your traps from yesterday? Zane asked in a quiet voice.

"Yes, I have the triggers here," Joseph replied, opening his bag.

"You have bait?" Zane whispered.

Joseph looked at his father and nodded.

"You and Ty circle around to the left. Set traps as you go, nothing fancy, okay? I'll meet you where the creek comes out of the lake around sunup."

"Do I get to set some of the traps?" Ty asked.

"Set as many as you like but listen to Joseph, and I would like you to be at the creek before the sun hits the meadow, okay, guys?"

"Okay," Joseph said.

"Sure thing," Ty agreed.

Joseph and Ty slipped off around the left side of the meadow. Stopping occasionally, they set deadfalls and snares for small animals. The boys followed the tree line, sometimes going a little way into the timber and sometimes going out into the meadow. They moved as quickly as they dared, making as little noise as possible. They arrived at the creek as dawn was overtaking the meadow. After looking around for their father, the boys enjoyed a long cool drink and washed their hands and faces.

The world was coming alive around them. The day creatures of the meadow were waking up, the night creatures going home. Fish hunted the calm water eddies in the stream, and birds, singing of abundant pleasures, flitted about in the trees around them. Every creature of the meadow was eager for another spring day. Joseph and Ty lay down in the sun next to the creek and watched the thick mist fade from the water, becoming a wisp of nothing, revealing a mirror image of the surrounding timber in the cold mountain lake.

"What do you think we're going to do today?" Ty asked, leaning on his left elbow to look at Joseph.

"I don't know, but I bet we go after that elk."

"Yeah, I forgot about the elk." Ty's eyes opened wide, and he fixed his gaze beyond Joseph.

"What is it?" Joseph asked.

"There is a rabbit under a bush about fifteen feet behind you."

"Don't look right at it, or he'll know you spotted him."

Ty concentrated his eyes on the ground about four feet in front of the rabbit. His peripheral vision kept watch on the young cottontail.

"Is he still there?" Joseph asked, forcing his voice to sound calm.

"Yeah, he hasn't moved." Ty felt like the sound of his heart beating was going to scare the rabbit. His breaths came in short draws and everything but the rabbit became a blur in his mind.

"I'm going to sit up. Then you stand up and throw. If you move too fast, he'll bolt."

Joseph sat up slowly.

Ty stood and threw his spear in a casual fluid motion. His fingers felt like they reached out to touch his prize. At the last moment he saw the surprise in the rabbit's eyes. The spear flew straight and pierced the rabbit through the middle, pinning it to the ground.

"Yes!" Ty yelled and ran up and grabbed the shaft of the spear as the rabbit kicked at the ground, screaming like a frightened child. The young rabbit screamed and clawed the ground in a desperate attempt to pull itself free. Ty grabbed it close to its neck and pinned it down, then drew his knife. Holding the base of the antler handle, he sharply struck the top of the rabbit's head with the back of the knife. The animal froze for an instant, then kicked loosely at the air as his spirit released into the world, and he lay lifeless in Ty's hand.

Ty felt a moment of sorrow as the rabbit fell silent, then a rush of exhilaration. On past hunts, Ty had seen his dad throw spears at rabbits, and he had missed each of those. But Ty had done it. He had speared a rabbit.

"Good throw," Joseph said, putting his hand on his brother's shoulder. "Dad couldn't have done any better."

"Thanks. I got him," Ty said, looking up at his brother.

The two boys just stood there grinning at each other.

"Are we having fun or what?" Joseph said.

The two boys started laughing, trying desperately not to make too much noise.

Zane watched as his sons enjoyed the first rays of sun on the water. Then he saw Ty stand and throw his spear and scream while running to a nearby bush. Then he trotted over to find out what had happened.

"Nice job with that, Ty," Zane said, standing over the boys.

Joseph and Ty were startled out of their revelry. They hadn't seen or heard their father walk up.

"Yep, I got him," Ty said, recovering with a smile.

"Good throw. I was fifteen before I got my first rabbit with a spear."

"You got a raccoon," Joseph exclaimed, seeing a large raccoon on the ground where they had been lying when they had first seen the rabbit.

"He was walking downstream. I chased him into the meadow. I could have used a spear then. He turned to fight, and I took him with my throwing stick. He was a brave fighter." He showed the boys a vicious tear on the top of his blood-soaked right hand.

"Let's take a bath, then we'll cook some food, and you guys can tell me about that elk," Zane said.

"Is your hand okay?" Joseph asked.

"I'm fine."

"Take a bath?" Ty said. "I already washed my face."

Joseph smiled. He knew Ty was going to hate this.

"No complaints," Zane said sternly. "If you complain, you'll stand out there until you convince me you love it."

"I'm not complaining," Ty said sheepishly.

The three naked males walked into the lake to above their knees. Zane knelt and scrubbed his body and face vigorously, then dunked his head, shaking it under water. Throwing his head back, he stripped the water from his face and backward off his hair with his hands. The boys reached down and grabbed handfuls of water to splash themselves, desperately hoping they wouldn't have to kneel, too.

"There, doesn't that feel better?" Zane asked, walking back toward shore.

"Oh, I feel better." Joseph shivered with a smile. "How about you, Ty? Do you feel better?"

"Oh, yeah, I feel great." Ty answered unconvincingly and looking a little blue.

Zane and his sons dressed and built a fire. Zane slit the rabbit's belly from between the rear legs to between the front legs, careful not to cut through into the stomach or chest cavity. Then he pulled the skin off by working his fingers along the fascia tissue between the flesh and the hide until the skin was only connected around its feet and head. Zane broke the feet sideways, cut them free from the body and skin, and then cut the head off at the base of the skull.

With the hide, feet, and head removed, he gutted the rabbit, cleaned it in the stream and skewered it on a long stick ready for cooking. Zane took greater care with the raccoon pelt, skinning it neatly around the face and feet. While he removed the hides, the boys gathered firewood and prepared a spit to roast the rabbit and raccoon.

"This raccoon is huge," Joseph said, stretching the skin out on a rock to pull and scrape the last bit of tissue from the hide.

"He was a good thirty-five pounds," Zane said. "He was a big old man. We needed it. We won't have much time for hunting for the next couple days."

Zane cut roasting sticks and skewers from the nearby brush, then sat down to prepare the food for the fire. He slid the rabbit onto a long shaft that had been whittled smooth, except for a small four-inch long sharpened branch in the middle. With the rabbit slid onto the stick, the small, sharpened branch skewered it into place. Additional small sticks pinned the front and back legs together and the body of the rabbit tight to the roasting stick. The rabbit would remain firmly in place as the stick was turned over the flame, cooking the meat evenly on all sides.

The raccoon was cut into roasting size pieces and impaled onto three-foot long sticks. The rabbit was skewered across the center of the fire ring and the pieces of raccoon leaned against the larger shaft that held the rabbit. The cooking meat tented the small fire in the center. An abundant pile of broken branches sat to the side, ready to be fed into the fire as needed.

"Now, tell me about that elk," Zane said as he sat down and fed the fire a couple of small sticks.

"It was really something, Dad," Ty began. "It was like he lay down to rest and got froze in."

"That's right, Dad. I couldn't see where anything else killed him. He's a spike. I think it was his first winter; maybe his second."

Zane looked at his sons with pride. "That's great, guys! After we have something to eat, I want to make some fish traps. This creek is full of brook trout. Then we'll take a look at this elk."

Joseph stretched out the rabbit skin, careful not to tear the delicate hide. Zane removed the brain from both the rabbit and raccoon, and he set them aside so he could use them to tan the hides.

"I'll cut some sticks for the fish traps," Joseph said, washing his hands and knife in the creek.

"I'll help," Ty volunteered eagerly.

"Why don't you watch this meat, Ty?" Zane said. "I'll go get material to tie the traps together."

"We could just set it back from the fire," Ty began. He looked at his father and stopped. "Okay, I'll watch the fire," he agreed with obvious disappointment. The last thing he wanted to do was hang around doing the cooking.

Ty looked over at Joseph. Joseph shrugged his shoulders and smiled, then trotted off downstream, looking for a stand of willow or other suitable sticks for fish traps.

"Cook it all well done, Ty. Turn it often so you don't burn it too bad, okay, son?" Zane said with his hand on Ty's shoulder. "I saw some cottonwood trees about a mile from here yesterday. I should be back in about an hour or so. When the meat is done, you can help Joseph. We need about sixty sticks. Cut them three feet long and thick as your little finger. If you find any good arrow shafts, keep them separate, okay?"

Ty started getting excited. Arrows meant bows. Bows meant real hunting. Ty liked all the other stuff. He was proud of his Nez Perce heritage. He was eager to learn everything his dad could teach him. But what he really liked was the hunt . . . the hunt and the shot. He wished it was like the olden days, so he could let the women take care of the cooking and tanning and all that stuff.

"Okay, Dad," Ty replied. "Are we going to make bows today?"

"Tomorrow," Zane answered. "Don't cut too much from one place, okay?"

"I wouldn't, Dad."

Eleven

"Have fun," Zane said, smiling at his young son.

Zane trotted away at a comfortable pace, feeling totally at ease. He jogged across the uneven ground, never looking at his feet, always aware of the world around him.

Ty cooked the meat. Paying close attention, he worked fast to feed the fire and turn the skewer sticks to evenly cook the meat. It was a chore to keep the fire fed while keeping the flame low enough to not burn the food.

Ty had helped work the fire since the first day he had gone out with his father. Even though he was not the best, he did a pretty good job when he had no distractions. It was pleasant work. The wet and cold from the morning bath turned into dry and toasty warm as he worked around the fire. The front of his legs became almost too warm as he knelt close, adjusting the stands of meat.

It always surprised him how little he thought about the cold when there were things to do. But it was a wonderful change when he became truly warm and dry again.

The smell of the roasting meat tugged at Ty's appetite as the food turned a golden brown above the coals and drifting smoke. After an hour or so, all of the meat looked well done. Ty cut into the fattest raccoon leg to check it. He took everything but the big legs off the fire and leaned the cooked meat against a tall rock. The last pieces cooked a while longer before he set them back away from the fire.

Joseph returned, carrying a bundle of sticks under his arm.

"That looks good. I'm hungry," Joseph said, laying down his sticks.

"I am, too. Do you think Dad would mind if we ate without him?"

"I don't think so," Joseph responded. "There's plenty. Let's save the rabbit for him, okay?"

"Sure." Ty liked the idea of saving his rabbit for Dad. Besides, he'd never eaten raccoon before. "How many sticks did you get?"

"About forty."

Ty cut a piece of meat from a skewer and tore off a bite.

"This raccoon is pretty good; it's a little tough, though." Ty said, grinning from his greasy, charcoal-smeared mouth. "Dad said we're going to make bows,"

"That sounds good to me. I got six or seven good arrow shafts," Joseph replied, sounding like he had expected the news.

"Dad said we need about sixty sticks besides our arrows," Ty continued.

"Do you know where he went?"

"To check out some cottonwood trees. He should be back in a little bit," Ty answered.

Joseph nodded like he knew what that meant.

Ty nodded back, pretending he knew, too.

When the boys finished the last of their meal, Joseph said, "Let's get the rest of those sticks."

Joseph and Ty headed out across the meadow together, collecting branches from bushes along the way.

. . .

As Zane approached the cottonwood trees, he saw a large buck browsing away from him. He automatically slipped into some cover and crept silently along behind the deer. After about ten minutes, he had cut the distance between them to about thirty yards. *If I were hunting, I could have you, old man,* Zane thought.

Leaving the deer to forage along oblivious of the near life and death moment, Zane walked through the old grove of trees until he saw what he was looking for. A large, old tree had fallen. It had stood at the edge of a seasonal creek. One hundred years of erosion and then a hard wind had pushed it over, leaving only half its roots still submerged in the earth. Some of the branches had new, green leaves while some were no longer fed by their airborne roots but still had their bark attached. Zane examined the dead branches. They had starved slowly, leaving them well cured with no cracks.

These will do fine, Zane thought. He cut four branches free with his knife. Three would make bows, and one long straight one would form a spear. With two staves in each hand, Zane trotted back toward the creek.

Joseph spotted his father at a distance and returned to stripping the bark from the sticks he'd picked for arrow shafts. When Zane arrived at the creek, the boys had a large pile of sticks laid aside and several long straight branches between them that they were working on. The cooked meat leaned against the spit away from the smoldering fire.

"Are those going to be the bows?" Ty asked as his father walked toward him.

He regretted asking even before the words cleared his mouth. All his life, he had been around his father and his father's friends. He had been told endless times that, if he was patient and observant, he would receive the answer to his questions. The world sometimes moved too slowly for Ty. Sometimes he had questions, and he wanted to be told the answer without having to think about it.

"You guys ready to make fish traps?" Zane said, not answering Ty.

"All set," Joseph said, sliding off his rock and setting his arrows aside.

"Me, too," Ty agreed, realizing his father did not want to talk about the bows right now.

"Good. Ty, would you divide up the sticks? The exact number isn't important. This stream isn't very large. So, we don't need to make big traps."

Joseph and Ty sat down next to their father. Ty handed his father the cooked rabbit.

"Here's your breakfast," Ty said proudly, handing the warm, golden-brown rabbit to his father.

"Thanks, Ty. This looks great. Don't you want to eat your rabbit?" Zane asked as he accepted the first food he'd eaten in thirty-six hours.

"We had some of the raccoon," Ty said with pride. "We saved this for you."

"That is very nice of you. I like the raccoon fine, but it is hard to beat the taste of a tender young rabbit." Zane washed his hands in the creek and sprinkled a little water on the dry flesh of the Rabbit. He took a small leather pouch out of his bag and carefully sprinkled a little salt onto the dampened meat. Then he sat down on the soft earth, leaned back against a sun-warmed granite boulder and enjoyed his perfectly cooked meal.

Both Ty and Joseph made mental notes to use the salt from the pouches in their shoulder bags on their next meals.

Ty told his dad the details of seeing the rabbit, how the throw had gone down and about how excited he was for everything they were going to be doing.

Zane enjoyed the warm meadow, the reflection of the mountains in the lake, and the sound of Ty's voice.

Joseph organized the sticks and continued to strip the arrow shafts.

With a full belly and a task at hand, Zane began the lesson of building fish traps.

"First you bind one end of your sticks," Zane demonstrated, taking a long strip of bark from the creek. He wrapped around four times, two inches up from the end of the bundle, added a couple of half hitches, then pulled the end of the strip through the bundle and cut off the excess strip.

Joseph and Ty watched and then copied their dad.

Zane, Joseph, and Ty weaved their traps, fueled by the conversation and the timeless labor while also basking with company from the world around them.

When the cone-shaped traps were finished, they anchored them under cut banks in the creek. The large end of the traps pointed upstream, waiting patiently to gather trout from the gently meandering stream. Pleased with their work, Zane and his sons looked forward to the sweet taste of a pink meat brook trout.

Walking back toward camp, they collected a gray squirrel and a ground squirrel from the boy's traps. An air of confidence settled over the three hunters. Food was no longer a concern.

Zane put everything that needed to stay cool into the wickiup. Joseph stretched the skins out flat on top of the granite boulder, with the other hides. Ty stowed the bow staves inside the wickiup, carefully setting one a little way away from the others.

"Joseph, would you lay the squirrels out up there to dry? Tomorrow we'll need to set up a drying rack. You can use this to pin it open so it will dry evenly," Zane said, tossing Joseph a small branch.

Ty and Zane tied all but three pieces of meat to the ceiling inside the wickiup. The three men sat down to eat a midday meal.

"Are we going to get the elk now?" Ty asked excitedly.

"At least part of it," Zane replied. "What kind of shape it's in will tell us how much we can use? We won't take any meat because it may have thawed during the winter and spoiled. But if the hide isn't bad, we'll take some of that. Then we'll take the brain to tan the hide, then the antlers and as many of the tendons as we can reach. We'll also get some hoofs and teeth. If he has any fat, we could use that, too."

"How long will that take?" Ty asked.

"It should only take a few hours. But it depends. If it is frozen tight to the ice it could take longer."

"It's in great shape, Dad," Ty said.

"Yeah, Dad, he looks like he could walk away if he wasn't frozen in."

"Well, let's go take a look," Zane said, standing up.

"Let's go," Ty agreed, picking up his spear and leading the way out of camp.

Ty led the way to the meadow where he and Joseph had seen the wolves. A shudder ran through his shoulders as he looked at the bush that had held the rabbit. I'm no cottontail, Ty thought as he trotted across the meadow, his spear cradled comfortably in his right hand.

When they reached the beginning of the second valley, Ty dropped back and let Joseph take the lead. Joseph led the way to the second meadow, and then up onto the snow field.

"There he is," Joseph said.

Ty and Zane walked up and stood beside him.

"Yep, there he is. Right where I found him," Ty said.

The young elk stared back with hollow black eyes. Flies buzzed around his nose and ears. His head rested comfortably against the log next to him.

"You were right, he's beautiful," Zane said, reaching down to feel the elk's side. "I've never seen an elk whose tongue didn't drop when he died. He must have died easy and froze fast. He's still frozen solid inside. If we needed to, we could probably eat him. Okay, guys, let's get to work. We need to clean the snow out from this side of him." Zane began to chop the icy snow in front of the elk with his knife, breaking off chunks and throwing them aside.

Joseph and Ty pitched in by chopping, pulling, and tossing the ice behind them. Then they scooped the corned snow beneath the top crust and flung it aside.

The elk was slowly freed from its frozen grave. It appeared to be lying down beside the log with its legs tucked under it. Twenty minutes of work cleared a path around the elk two feet wide and nearly to the earth where the elk lay on top of a layer of ice and snow.

"That wasn't too bad," Zane said, standing up and brushing off his clothes. "We are lucky the snow has melted down. When he died, I bet he was covered over. He was young and strong, but he should have stayed with an older cousin for his first winter. If he would have taken the time to dig another eight inches down to the earth, he might have held enough warmth to survive the storm. He was tucked in next to this log to block the wind and so the snow would blow over him.

"He had protection from the worst of the cold but the exposure from below was too much. It is a delicate balance in the cold. When you make a wrong decision, the cold can lull you to sleep, and the scavengers find your body in the spring thaw. We honor him for his gift of tools, and we are privileged to share his struggle in the world.

"We are going to take the hide first. We will cut across the body near the log, then over the top of the back and down the side that we cleared, then across the body again. You guys start on the other side then over his back. We will get most of this side."

Joseph and Ty cut across the frozen hide as low to the log as they could. Hair fell in bunches as they pressed their weight onto the backs of their knives. The stiff skin resisted any pressure. Zane worked his knife across the front, close to the ground. The body was still completely frozen down low. It was hard work, even for Zane. Next, the boys cut over the top while he worked up the sides to complete the square.

"Okay, let's see if we can pull it off," Zane said, working up one of the far corners.

Joseph lifted another corner, leaving Ty to slice the hide free, as Zane and Joseph pulled. It was stiff but not completely frozen. Once it got going, it peeled away from the carcass easily, leaving a naked elk with its legs comfortably folded beneath it. It was a strange sight. The young half-naked bull elk slumbered in the lee of the log. Joseph almost made a nervous remark, but he knew that he should keep it to himself. This sight would live in his memory for the rest of his life.

"You guys get the brain, antlers, and all of the front teeth. Use rocks to break them free; it will be easier."

Joseph picked up a rock a little bigger than his fist. Ty held the head steady while Joseph broke a hole in the skull at the base of the antlers. A sickening odor wafted out from the head of the elk.

"Oh, man," Joseph said, standing back.

"Yeow, that smells bad," Ty agreed, stepping back, too.

"Nothing smells like ripe brains." Zane smiled, picking up Joseph's rock.

Zane hit the head several more times, breaking the skull into pieces. He lifted the antlers still connected to a piece of bone and tossed them onto the hide. Then Zane reached in and lifted out the brain, which he tossed into the snow next to the hide. He filled the skull cavity with snow and washed his hands and knife in the icy crystals.

Ty had removed all the front teeth, uppers, and lowers, and put them into his pouch. "What are these teeth for?" he asked.

"Decorations for clothing and things," Zane replied. "We'll take them home."

Ty looked at the teeth, shrugged his shoulders and closed his bag.

"Now let's see if we can push him over," Zane said.

Zane, Joseph, and Ty got on the far side of the elk and pushed as hard as they could. Digging into the snow with their feet, they gave their best effort. The elk was happy where he was, frozen solid to the earth.

"Let's take the hooves and tendons from these legs," Zane said, walking around the snow to the free side of the elk.

Zane and his sons cut the tendons from the nearest legs, then tunneled under to the legs on the other side and cut the tendons from them. Zane carried the brain wrapped up in the hide. The hooves and tendons were stowed in his bag, while Joseph carried the antlers. They walked quietly back to camp.

Twelve

Back at camp Zane examined the dog tracks from the night before. They were clearly coyotes. He cut three long thin straps from the elk hide. At the edge of their small camp clearing, Zane fashioned three T-bar snares. Baiting them with squirrel entrails and raccoon scraps. Then he scattered the area with the bones left from the boys' breakfast.

If you come back tonight, you'll warm my back, Zane thought as he admired his deadly ambush.

After washing in the lake, Zane and his sons rested close to the fire.

"Are we going to make our bows tomorrow?" Ty asked, burying his teeth into a nicely charred raccoon leg.

"That is the plan. Tomorrow we'll start our bows and tan these skins. That was quite a throw on that rabbit this morning, Ty."

Ty shifted his position. Zane saw his son's chest swell with pride. "Yeah, I sure got him."

Zane and his sons talked about past trips. They savored one another's company, laughing and telling stories, acting out past hunts, pushing, and playing, drunk with freedom. For Zane and his sons, these times of reflection and storytelling carried some of life's greatest moments. In the glory, pain, and pleasure of a man's life, so many of the best times are spent around the fire with the people that you love and respect.

When the fire receded to coals, Zane put the small skins into the wickiup. He then placed the elk skin with the pungent brain on top of the granite boulder. Joseph and Ty handed up rocks to cover it over to keep it from being dragged away.

"I'm ready for bed," Zane said, leaning the two spears next to the door of the wickiup. "If we hook up one of those coyotes, they'll be mean." Zane leaned in and pulled out one of the staves from inside the wickiup. "Keep them back with the spears until I get him down. A big coyote could hurt you bad," he said, looking down at Ty.

"Don't worry." Ty's expression said he remembered the wolves all too clearly. "I'll be careful." His mind raced back to the two wolves snarling and tearing at each other. *Maybe they won't come,* Ty thought as he drifted into the oblivious sleep of youth.

The pack leader's nose tested the breeze. There was something in the air. Wending their way, the four coyotes traveled haphazardly through the dark trees. Like death looking for life's stragglers, they traveled with an air of disinterest.

The four silent thieves converged on the camp circle then cautiously slipped in. The area was alive with edible smells. The scent that drew them in was up high. The leader didn't like it; too many things didn't seem right. He hadn't lived this long by taking chances.

Smelling the wickiup, he circled back and sat down. Something was wrong, his hackles rose on his neck. The old female and her year-old pup nosed around the fire, picking up scraps, ignoring, but staying clear of their irritable leader. The two-year-old male circled wide around the dominant male, eating one small bone then another. The ground was littered with tasty morsels. The dominant male decided to stay clear of the wickiup and the rock pile. There were other things to be eaten away from this risky area.

The not so wise younger male lunged for another bite. A touch on the bait, a flip of a branch, and a noose was tightly bound around the coyotes' front leg. He leapt backward, almost colliding with the female and her pup, and started to run. The leader made the trees and looked back to see his comrade running back and forth. The lead coyote then saw a shadow move out of a pile of branches.

The trapped coyote snarled and tore at the air with a viciousness known only to those who are accustomed to bringing death. Then, he calmly backed into the brush. A lifetime of struggle for his daily survival had prepared him for this day. He was ready. He had fought many times before.

Zane heard the snare trip and the coyote fight against the leather tether. He had to move fast before the coyote chewed through the strap. Bursting through the entrance, Zane leapt to his feet. With the moon-bright night, he could see well enough. Zane looked toward the staff. Passing it by, he pulled his knife and approached the bushes that held his snares.

The coyote growled, backing deeper into the bush, pulling his tether with him. Protected on both sides and behind.

As Zane cautiously moved toward the traps, he could hear the other coyotes moving nervously beyond the edge of his clear vision.

Zane approached to ten feet from his quarry, then stopped to evaluate. He was a large coyote, fully sixty pounds. He clearly wasn't trying to run. He had dug in, pulling the snare with him. The strap would leave him free movement, out even as far as Zane was now. This coyote was clever.

Zane moved in, crouching low, arms fully extended, and staring directly into the fierce eyes of the snarling predator. The coyote lunged forward, and then quickly retreated. Zane inched forward. The coyote lunged again, ripping the air where Zane's hand had been. Zane slashed into space as his adversary bounced backward. Impending death focused the resolve of both warriors.

Zane sprung forward, then leaned back as the coyote flew for his throat. Zane dropped flat to the ground. His knife flashed upward, piercing the lung of the astonished coyote. The animal screamed, rolled once, and regained his feet. Zane and the coyote stood facing each other again.

A spear struck the side of the wounded animal. He jumped back, away from his new attacker, and the light spear fell away. Zane's right foot struck savagely upward into the coyote's throat. Then his knife found its mark, and the mighty predator was tamed by Zane's steel tooth. The other coyotes in the shadows turned and disappeared into the night.

"That was awesome!" Ty and Joseph shouted as they ran over to their father.

Zane looked over to his sons and saw Joseph carrying his cottonwood stave.

"That was a good throw, Joseph. If you had a point on your spear, you would have put him down."

"Why didn't you throw, Ty?" Zane asked.

"Joseph told me not to. He said I should watch for the rest of the pack," Ty protested.

"He was right." Zane said, "If you're not ready for the unexpected, one day you could find yourself in a bigger fight than you bargained for."

"He is beautiful, isn't he?" Zane asked, stroking the coyote's winter coat. "His friends will be sorry to lose such a fierce companion."

"Let's get the fire going. We won't get any more sleep tonight."

Joseph and Ty put down their spears and blew the fire into life.

"I'm getting tired of this raccoon," Ty said, munching on a cold piece of meat.

Joseph and Zane looked at Ty, who was giving full attention to his breakfast.

"Maybe we'll get some trout this morning," Joseph said with a smile.

"It's going to be a busy day," Zane said while preparing an area to skin the coyote. "A sweet brook trout would be a tasty start, wouldn't it?"

Ty smiled, and nodded, fighting with the urge to ask if they could go to check the traps now.

Zane worked meticulously on the coyote hide, being careful not to cut holes in the skin. It was a beautiful thick winter coat scarred from a lifetime of life and death struggle. He took the four largest teeth and put them in his bag. Then removed the brain, fat, and large tendons and laid them aside.

Zane added wood to the fire and moved several fist-size rocks into the coals. Joseph and Ty gathered the skins, including the elk hide. They also pulled out the brains they had saved for the tanning and put them on the coyote pelt. They left the elk brain on top of the granite rock, avoiding its rancid smell.

Zane and his sons walked to the lake, weighted the elk hide with rocks until it was completely under water, then washed their hands and faces and drank their fill. A crisp star-filled sky that surrounded them. With only about an hour left till dawn, the night birds and crickets sang a chorus accompanied by a lone frog singing for a mate.

There was no cold wind to drive them back to the trees this morning. It was still crisp, but they were more accustomed to the cold now. More comfortable than they had been when they first arrived. The three looked at each other, smiling broadly.

"Thank you, Lord," Joseph said.

"Amen," answered Ty and Zane.

They walked back to camp, carrying some water in the raccoon skin.

Near the fire they laid the raccoon skin in the middle of a ring of stones making a bowl with one-half inch of water covering the bottom. All the brains were placed in with the water and mashed into a paste with their fists. They warmed the mixture by adding fire-warmed rocks, being careful not to overheat and cook the tanning solution. Finally, the paste was spread thinly over the skin side of each of the pelts, carefully working into the edges. After hours of hard work, the liquid had been evenly pressed and rubbed into all areas of the pelts.

"Coyotes stay well clear of an area where they smell a dead cousin. Our hides won't be touched if we leave camp, not by coyotes, anyway," Zane added.

"Let's go wash up and check our traps," Zane said, heading for the lake.

As Zane and his sons looked out into the meadow, they saw a deer with two fawns browsing their way toward the head of the lake.

"I can't believe our ancestors got to live here all the time," Ty said aloud.

"They still do," Zane said, walking toward the lake.

Thirteen

fter washing, they walked along the shore toward the meadow that held their traps.

"What did you mean when you said our ancestors still live here, Dad?" Ty asked.

"The spirit world is all around us, Ty. We're a part of it, and it is a part of us. Our connection with that part of nature is something the white man will never know and never understand. When the white men forced us from our land, they thought we had lost everything. But the spirit of a Nez Perce is never lost. We will hunt in these mountains until the white man cuts down the last tree."

They walked in silence the rest of the way to the meadow. They arrived as the last shadows of night were being driven into the trees. Zane and the boys quickly worked the land traps. They harvested a young rabbit. After moving some of the traps farther around the meadow and adding three snares, Zane and his sons returned to the head of the creek above their fish traps.

"Okay, guys; the idea is we wade downstream slowly. We'll push the fish from cover to cover until they hide in our trap. Then we pull it out."

"Sounds fun," Ty said.

"Sounds cold," Joseph added, smiling at his dad.

After taking off their boots and rolling up their pants, the three black haired, leather-clad fish herders worked their way downstream.

The first trap yielded nothing. The second trap gave them a beautiful nine-inch trout. The third produced four fish, each one about six inches long. They moved the three traps downstream, and two of the snares were reset with fish entrails for bait.

The three fish trappers walked briskly back toward camp. There would be trout for breakfast. After roasting their fish, the mood of the day was comfortable and relaxed as they enjoyed each morsel of pink flesh. They retold stories of slippery-footed fish headers and darting trout that zigged when they should have zagged. It was a different scene from the life and death struggle of a few hours before.

After breakfast, Joseph and Ty skinned the rabbit, storing the meat and the brains, fat, and tendons in the cool shade of the wickiup. The skin was laid out in the sun on the rocks. Zane pulled the three bow staves out of the wickiup. Examining each one carefully, he gave one to each of the boys and kept one. Ty's smile radiated with an inner joy after seeing that his dad had given him the one that he had earlier chosen for himself.

"Every bow maker has little things they do differently. But basically, you work either a rat tail, flat back, or a flat back with a slight cone shape for additional strength. My bow at home is Osage Orange wood with a flat back. With the kind of wood we are using, I prefer a flat back with a slight cone shaped belly because it has a little more power than the flat back or rat tail. These staves are good medium quality dry wood. If you were to shape it like mine, I don't think you could pull it; so, I suggest you both do a rat tail design."

"Okay, Dad," Joseph and Ty both agreed.

"First remove the bark, then we will cut the length. Stand it up with the small end down. Mark your stave at the middle of your chest. If you make it longer, it will throw farther and be a little bit more forgiving. A longer bow rides too high on your back and gets tangled in the brush. A shorter bow is better for shooting from horseback and for not getting tangled in the brush, but they don't throw as far. Now we need to find the middle and mark the grip. Don't groove deep. Mark the spot. Make the grip area about one half inch longer than your hand.

"Next, put the large end down and your right hand on top. Put your left hand on the grip and pull it around in a small circle. Can you feel that one way it flexes a little easier?" he asked. Once the boys nodded, he continued. "Mark the side that your stave is flexing from. That will be the belly of your bow. I use a small x to mark the belly side on the line that marks my handle. Now put your knives away. That is the last time you will touch your knife to your bow. In your pouches is a large piece of obsidian."

Ty and Joseph each pulled a piece of obsidian out of their pouches. They were thick flakes, about one inch deep and the size of their fists.

"If you use your knives to carve away wood from your bow, your bow will lose strength. Use the obsidian at a right angle from the wood and shave off the excess wood. We need to shape the bow, gracefully tapering it down to the tip, which should end up about the thickness of your finger. This is a long job. We also need to work these skins today. Be patient. Relax into the perfection of each movement. The old men used to take a week or more to make a bow. Some of them were beautiful works of art. Start on the smaller side, then match the larger one to it."

Joseph and Ty started their task. It seemed enormous.

Ty glanced at Joseph after about twenty minutes of work that left no visible change in the size of his bow. Joseph worked away with an excited and focused look in his eyes. Ty could see that it would be no use trying to talk to him now. There were times that Joseph seemed divided between this world and another. Ty watched as Joseph, in even strokes, sent long curls of wood gliding down the limb of his bow.

Finally, Ty relaxed and resigned himself to his own labor. Concentrating on each stroke, long even shavings started to gather around his feet.

Zane watched his sons until they appeared to be working comfortably. Then he sat down with his spear stave. First, he removed all of the bark. Then, like the boys, he used a piece of obsidian to smooth the seven-foot stave. With long, even strokes, he smoothed off the gray outer wood, leaving a round, even pole slightly tapering from one inch to one and one quarter at the heavier end.

"Okay, guys." Zane said, "let's put these away for now. We need to get to the skins."

The boys reluctantly put down their bows. After brushing off the litter of shavings, they stretched their legs and backs. The first half on both bows was close to shaped. The boys inspected their handiwork with pride. They had looked forward to this day for years. Soon, they would have a bow like their fathers. All the staves were carefully placed into the shade of the wickiup.

"The idea," Zane began, "is to rub the paste into the skin until it's dry. If you push too hard, you can tear the smaller ones. You can use your hands to do some of the rubbing. I would suggest, though, that you mostly use a smooth rock in the large areas and a smooth, round-ended stick in the small places. Sometimes, a little sand helps to work the leather when you feel it's almost done."

Zane folded over the bottom few inches of the coyote skin and knelt on the fur. Then he took a smooth-edged, oblong rock about one and a half times the size of his fist from his bag. Zane had taken the rock from the creek this morning for this purpose. Holding the rock in both hands, he pushed in long strokes across the hide.

Joseph and Ty searched the area, found suitable rubbing tools and went to work. After about twenty minutes of working on the squirrel skin, Ty carried it over to his father.

"How's this, Dad?"

Zane took the pelt and examined it. The skin felt clammy, and the edges looked damp. "This looks good. When it's finished, it will feel warm to the touch. The edges should look as finished as the middle."

Zane worked steadily on the coyote all afternoon, alternating between working the middle and the edges with a methodical, steady pace, spending as little energy as possible in each stroke. He finished the pelt from the tip of the tail up through the head. At the head, Zane worked along, inch by inch. With a round-ended stick, he worked with the skill of a taxidermist.

By late afternoon, the boys had finished all the small skins and Zane had the raccoon well rubbed down.

"Let's put this away for today," Zane said, folding the raccoon in half then rolling it up.

"My hands are dead." Ty said.

"So are mine," Joseph said, looking at his tired hands like they would never work again.

"Think what the women used to feel like after a buffalo hunt," Zane said, rubbing his hands together then stretching his back. "Let's go wash up. Then we can take a walk and check our traps."

As they traveled the short distance to the lake, the fatigue fell away from their bodies. Only their hands still felt the weariness from the day's labor.

"I wish we could stay here for a month," Ty said, shifting his spear to under his arm, and balancing it across his forearm. "How long before we have to start heading out?"

"I don't know," Zane answered. "My definite plans don't go beyond making our bows."

"Aren't we going to use the sweat lodge?" Joseph asked.

"We will before we leave."

Ty wanted to say something, just to talk. He was excited about getting into the sweat lodge and feeling truly warm and clean again. He missed regular things like helping his mom in the kitchen. He missed how they would joke and laugh together. He missed hearing her singing when he came home from school. Sometimes, Ty thought Joseph and Dad were too serious when they were in the woods. They acted like this was the olden days.

Ty understood, if he tried, that Joseph was not only learning the skills of their forefathers, but he was also learning to think like them. He wanted that, too, but sometimes Ty just wanted to be Ty. And right now, he missed his mom.

Fourteen

When they reached the lake, they drank their fill, washed themselves in the cold water, and then sat by the bank to enjoy the view.

There were still a couple of hours of sunlight left in the day. In a gentle breeze, the reflection from the snow-covered ridges to the west cast a brilliant reflection shimmering across the lake.

Zane took in the scene. "It's like the world is brand new. Before the white man came, the winter would cleanse the world, making it fresh for the new beginnings of spring. Like this place is now. One day, we'll walk those mountains with our ancestors. We'll hunt buffalo on the prairies. And we'll count coup on our neighbors, the Bannock. Each spring the earth will be fresh with a new year," he finished in little more than a whisper.

Joseph looked at his father. He knew Zane believed what he had said, but his words made no sense to Joseph.

"I'm going to work on the elk hide. You guys check the traps. Pick up everything but the fish traps. Leave those alone. We'll check them tomorrow, okay?"

"Okay," Joseph said as he and Ty headed off toward the meadow.

Zane pulled the elk hide out of the lake. He laid it flat on the grass with the hair up. Scraping it with his knife, the hair fell out easily. After about a half hour, Zane rinsed it off then scraped it a little more. Then he wrung it out the best he could and carried it back to camp. After draping the hide over a limb to drain, Zane gathered firewood and then set about preparing the evening meal.

Joseph and Ty went a new way to the meadow. They walked straight out from the lake, then up onto the ridge that bordered the meadow on the southeast side. Walking slowly and carefully, they came upon a doe feeding its way up the ridge.

Joseph signaled his brother to stay put, so Ty dropped down onto his knees. Joseph set down his spear and carefully crept toward the deer. He started his approach about forty-five yards away. In five minutes, he closed the distance to thirty yards.

The doe sharply lifted its head to look around.

Joseph froze in mid-stride. Maintaining his gaze at the ground behind the doe, Joseph held his position like a statue. After about ten minutes of testing the wind and scanning the area for movement, the deer resumed her browsing. Joseph moved forward to a bush about fifteen yards away. Crawling silently through the brush, Joseph lay flat on the ground some twenty feet from the deer. She browsed and nibbled while moving up the ridge. He watched her feed toward him, angling to a trail about six feet in front of his position.

The deer stepped forward onto the trail. Joseph eased out straight behind the deer. He took three quick steps, lifted his hand to touch the deer, and stepped on a twig. The deer bolted out from under his hand as he swung it down into space. The deer ran off, leaving Joseph grinning behind it.

"That was awesome!" Ty yelled, running up behind Joseph. "You got her! You counted coup on a deer!"

"I was so close," Joseph said, still grinning in the direction of the long-gone deer. "I missed her by an inch. I could feel her hair move out from under my hand, but I didn't touch her. I was this close," Joseph said, showing Ty an inch between his fingers.

"That was the most incredible stalk I've ever seen," Ty said, handing Joseph his spear. Ty didn't think he could have admired his big brother anymore, but at this moment he looked at him like he was a full-grown man.

Both boys stood grinning at the spectacle of it in their minds. Turning downhill, Joseph and Ty headed toward the meadow to see how their traps had done. The meadow was fresh with an evening breeze. A few squirrels chattered their last opinions of the day before slipping into the security of their nests. Joseph and Ty quickly walked the trap line, picking it up as they went. They found a jackrabbit that was twice the size of the bunnies they'd caught before, hanging from one of the snares. Joseph dispatched it and tucked it into his bag. They were getting short on daylight. The cold was starting to push up from the earth.

"Do you miss Mom?" Ty asked as Joseph worked on the large hare.

Joseph thought for a moment then answered. "I miss her a lot. Every day there are things I want to tell her. I miss her cooking, and I miss kissing her good night. But I'd stay out here all summer if I could. If Dad would let me, I'd even stay here by myself."

Ty looked at Joseph, a little stunned at the thought. "I miss her, too," said Ty. Then after a pause, he added, "I'd like to count coup on a deer before I go home, though. If I could."

The boys finished picking up the traps and trotted back to camp. Shortly after the last rays of light disappeared behind the ridgeline, Joseph and Ty walked up to the fire. Zane warmed some of the raccoon on the spit then held up a cooked squirrel to the boys.

"If you guys want to start on this, the rest should be ready in a few minutes."

The boys settled in around the fire, then set their attention on devouring their dinner.

"This jack will keep until tomorrow morning," Zane said, taking the rabbit from Joseph. After a while, Zane handed skewers of hot dripping meat to the boys.

"Joseph almost touched a deer," Ty said with his mouth full of food.

Zane smiled at Joseph, who smiled back and nodded.

"How close did you get?"

"I was about one inch away. I could feel her hair slip out from under my fingers, but I didn't touch her skin."

"Did she hear you?"

"When I stood up after my stalk, I took a few quick steps from behind her. On my last step, I made a noise, and she spooked."

"One inch, that counts. I've known a lot of good hunters that have never been able to stalk up close enough to touch a mule deer."

"Did you and Grandfather ever go on trips like this?" Ty asked after he finished the last scraps of his dinner.

"My father, your grandfather, died in Vietnam when I was two, so we never got to go out together. My grandfather taught me. I wish you could have met your great-grandfather. He was a remarkable man. His father fought beside Chief Joseph when we ran from the soldiers. My grandfather told me about it. It was a terrible time. The Nez Perce survived better than most because of the many great chiefs we've had and because there were men like your great grandfather, who remembered, and wouldn't let the old ways go untaught. My grandfather will always be my greatest hero."

Zane and his sons talked for a while about how life was and how they wished it could be.

"Dad, when we die, where do we go? Do we go to heaven or to a place that just has Indians or what?" Ty asked as he lit the end of a small stick and spun it around in the night sky.

"I don't know, Ty. When I die, I'll have to ask my grandfather that one," Zane answered with a smile. "I'm going to turn in, guys."

A cold wind moved through the trees, sending a chill down Joseph's back.

"Good idea," agreed the boys.

The next morning, Zane rolled out early. By first light he had built a drying rack for the remaining meat that they had harvested. When Joseph and Ty finally peeked out from the wickiup, Zane was rubbing the brain paste into the fire-warmed elk hide.

"That smells gross," Ty said, trying to stretch while holding his nose.

"Yeah, Dad, it's pretty bad."

Zane glanced up from his labor, looking like he hadn't noticed. "It is pretty bad, isn't it?" Zane said, looking at his sons. "If you guys want, you could go ahead to see if we have fish for breakfast."

"Okay, Dad," Ty said, picking up his spear and heading toward the lake.

"You've been busy," Joseph said, looking at the drying rack and the fire pit full of coals.

"You better stick with your brother. I still don't like him walking around alone."

Zane watched his son trot off to catch his brother. *I have some fine boys,* he thought as he returned to his work.

Ty was on his knees, washing his face and hands when Joseph trotted up and sat down next to him. Together they looked out over the sparkling water and across the snow fields that led up the rocky ridges.

"I hope I'll never forget these days," Joseph said.

"We won't," Ty answered.

Joseph and Ty took off their clothes and jumped into the water. Kicking and screaming, they scrubbed themselves, dunked their heads, and scrambled to the bank. After dressing they trotted over to the meadow that held their fish traps.

"Let's walk downstream to see if we can spear a rabbit," Ty suggested.

"That's fine. I don't think Dad would care if we took a little more time."

Off they went, one on each side of the creek, moving along slowly, looking for a rabbit in close cover. They saw a larger cotton tail at a distance, but he was an experienced survivor who would not so easily be found after being spooked. Young rabbits were a completely different game. Often when they spook, they run twenty feet, turn a corner, and hide under the first bush they find.

Joseph and Ty had seen their father arrow many rabbits, using a circular stalk on young rabbits. Joseph and Ty walked until they departed the meadow and stepped into a cold, steep-walled canyon. The rugged terrain and the dense timber held the cold and, more importantly, held no promise of game like their meadow did. So, the boys turned back to the more familiar open country and the warmth of the meadow that held their fish traps. Joseph and Ty waded up to each trap, finding them empty.

"We should have checked them first thing this morning," Joseph said after looking into the third empty trap.

"Should we move them or leave them here?"

"We'll move them."

After shifting the fish traps farther downstream, the boys made their way back to camp.

It had already been a long morning for Zane. The last of the raccoon and squirrel meat dried on the rack. The elk hide was finished on the fleshed side then stretched over a tree limb and hung up to air out. The two rabbits and the squirrel skins were also laid out with the paste applied to the flesh side. After the camp was in order, Zane went down to the lake to drink and bathe in the late morning sun.

These times are the best, Zane thought. *The only sounds are the voices of friends in the glory of life. The only pressures are for food and shelter. People have given up far more than they know for clean fingernails and hot showers.*

FIFTEEN

Zane walked back to camp and found his sons scraping away on their bows. There was no fish cooking, no fire going.

"Ty, would you cook that jackrabbit?"

"You bet, Dad. I'm starving," Ty said, setting his bow down and jumping to the task of preparing the rabbit.

"I'll make the fire," Joseph said, laying his bow aside.

"Great," Zane said, pulling his spear out of the wickiup.

Zane felt the length of the spear for smoothness and uniform shape. Feeling satisfied with his work, he used his knife to round the smaller end, and a stone to sand down rough edges left by the knife. Next, he took a leather pouch out of his shoulder bag. From the pouch, he took several pieces of partially worked flint wrapped in a square piece of leather. Laying the stones out neatly on the leather, Zane selected a long narrow spear point. He had rough shaped it at home, but it still needed work on the tip and edges.

Joseph and Ty watched their father tuck the piece of flint wrapped in elk hide into his left hand. Then he took a five-inch-long tip of a deer antler from his pouch and started flaking chips from the edge of the stone.

Zane worked with precise and focused pressure to break away unwanted thickness. First one side was finished, working toward the point, and then he turned the stone for the other edge. After twenty minutes, he had a beautifully shaped spear point, delicately tapered with razor-sharp edges, ending in a chisel tip about an eighth of an inch across. He examined it with satisfaction, then handed it to Joseph.

"This looks great," Joseph said, turning it over in his hand. He had been given a couple of stone napping lessons, but he had never come close to work like this.

Ty looked it over and said, "I can hardly wait until I can make things like that."

"It takes patience and practice. I'll give you a lesson tomorrow," Zane promised, taking the tip from Ty.

Zane then notched the spear to accept the point, carefully removing the wood so as not to split the spear beyond the notch. As he fit the tip into the end of the spear, Ty announced that the rabbit was ready. Putting down their work, Joseph and Zane joined Ty at the fire. Pulling the hot meat from the skewer, they quickly devoured the large rabbit. Every morsel was picked from the bones. Relaxing back with full stomachs, Zane looked at Ty and smiled.

"That was the best rabbit I've ever eaten."

"Yeah, Ty, it was great," agreed Joseph.

Ty looked at them and let loose a huge belch and smiled. They all roared with laughter. Zane and Joseph made valiant but futile attempts to better Ty's magnificent roar.

"You are the king." Zane laughed, finally giving up the contest.

"I would like to arrow a deer so we could have some venison, but I don't think that is going to happen on this trip," Joseph said to Ty.

"We could have got that one yesterday," Ty said excitedly, hoping his father would think it was a good idea, too.

"We could get one, Ty," Zane said. "That isn't the problem. The reason is, the does are still having fawns, and Idaho deer season doesn't start for another three months. Who knows, though? A lot could happen in the next ten days."

Joseph and Ty smiled. That was definitely not a "No way."

Joseph and Ty resumed work on their bows. Within half an hour Joseph asked his father to check his first side, then he started to work on the other half.

Zane finished the notch for the spearhead, then he tapered the last foot of the spear down to the notch. When he finished, the diameter at the notch was the same width as the body of the spear point. Now, he was ready to mount the point. He took the coyote tendons that he had left drying on the boulder with those that they'd taken from the elk. Separating groups of strands, Zane stripped them into several thin strings. With gentle pounding they became light, almost fluffy cords. Next, he placed some pine pitch on a flat rock in the fire. When it melted, he used a stick to smear it onto the inside of the notch. After bedding the point in the pitch, he carefully wrapped the point onto the end of the spear.

Zane inspected his work. Testing the balance, he lunged it into the air. He didn't have to throw it. He knew it would fly straight. It was long enough to throw, short enough to maneuver in the trees, and heavy enough to penetrate.

It is a beautiful spear, Zane thought. *The best I've ever made.* He leaned his spear against the wickiup and turned his attention to the unfinished skins.

The boys continued to work on their bows. Ty wanted to use his knife to speed things up, but his dad had said not to. He kept scraping, sending little curls of wood to pile up around his feet.

After a couple more hours, Joseph put down his bow and helped his father with the skins. By late afternoon, the last of them were finished.

"Dad, can I take a break?" Ty asked, rubbing his aching hands together.

"Of course, you can. I wouldn't mind getting out of camp myself. You guys up for a hike?"

"Yeah!"

"Me, too. I didn't know this would take so long."

Zane put his throwing stick into the pocket on the back of his shirt.

The boys took their spears, and they were off.

Zane led the way, heading east out of camp. This was new terrain. After a short distance of heavy timber, the landscape gave way to high rolling ridges, covered in chest high brush intermixed with a scattering of trees. Fresh deer tracks covered the narrow game trails. Within a half hour, Zane and his sons had jumped three deer from their beds.

"All right, guys, let's play a game. We split up and we each work our way to that rock outcropping on that small ridge. The one that sees the most deer within shooting range before they see you wins. We only have a couple of hours before dark, so be at the rock before sunset. Spear a rabbit if you can, but we are hunting these deer for practice, not for food, so leave them alone."

Ty and Joseph went out about seventy to eighty yards. One to each side of their father, they began to move slowly toward the rock outcropping. As the boys crept away, Zane lay down where he was and waited. After a half hour of silence, Zane started to slowly creep toward the outcropping, stopping every three or four feet to look slowly all around his position. In twenty minutes, Zane had traveled about seventy yards. Fixed on the smallest movements, he saw what he was looking for. A large mule deer buck with heavy, but short, newly budding antlers was crawling toward him.

The buck had no idea that he was being watched. He focused his attention in the direction that Ty had been heading. As the buck listened, his ears perked and turned toward a sound that Zane could only imagine. The deer's nose constantly tested the air, looking for clues to the identity of the predator that he sensed lurked no more than a moment's run away.

Zane knew Ty's identity was safe unless an unexpected breeze gave him away. After several moments the deer stood, secure that he was out of harm's reach. Zane slipped five feet forward to the edge of the bush that concealed him. He was twenty feet straight behind the buck, with only the edge of a bush concealing his outline.

Barely audible, Zane made the sound of a buck snort. The large buck turned carelessly and stood broadside to Zane, still unaware that under different circumstances this day would be his last. Uncomfortable that he couldn't see the other buck, the deer trotted briskly away.

After another hour, the three hunters met at the rock outcropping.

"I scared up two does almost right away, then I didn't see any more after that," Ty said.

"I saw them, too," Joseph interrupted. "Then later I heard one bounce off, so I did a fawn bleat. Then I think the same one snorted at me and ran off. I never did see it, so it could have been a buck or a doe."

"If it circled back because of a bleat, then it was probably a doe with fawn, or a barren doe that was feeling maternal. If you bleat at a moving doe, move about fifty yards down wind as quiet as you can, and wait. That is when you will get your shot."

Zane and his sons worked their way back to camp. Zane got a small squirrel with his throwing stick. They all foraged for edible greens and roots. The less tasty ones were passed over. This was no longer a trip of questionable survival. There was dried meat in camp.

Around the fire that night, Zane and his sons practiced their buck grunts, doe bleats, bird, and coyote calls. They spent most of the evening learning how to talk to their forest cousins.

SIXTEEN

The next morning, Joseph and Ty went to check the traps. Zane worked the skins over a branch to soften them up. By the time the boys arrived back with breakfast, Zane had finished the coyote and the raccoon.

After a breakfast of trout and watercress, the boys went to work on their bows. Zane started in on the elk hide. Within a couple of hours, it was workable leather, not soft enough for clothing but good enough for what Zane had in mind.

Dark clouds had been gathering steadily all morning. By early afternoon, it was obvious that a spring storm was on its way. Joseph finished his bow first. It looked like Ty was a few hours behind if he stayed with it. Zane helped Joseph heat the ends of his bow. Then they bent them over a rock and held them in place until set.

It was a beautifully shaped bow with delicately re-curved ends. Joseph got out the fat that had been saved from the animals they had eaten. Zane took some and started to rub it into the length of his spear. Joseph took half of the fat left and worked it into his bow. By the time they finished, Ty was adding the finishing touches to his bow.

Joseph helped Ty re-curve the ends. After it had been treated with fat, they cut strips from the elk hide to use as strings. The string was tied permanently to the bottom. The top would be secured with a couple of half hitches. Then the bows were drawn for the first time, and they bent like God had grown them for that purpose. The boys beamed with pride. Now all they needed were arrows.

"We had better do something about a more comfortable shelter. It is going to rain on us soon," Zane said, feeling the dampness in the air.

"Same stuff as before?" Ty asked.

"We will need some longer poles. I would like to build right over the fire area. We could lay them across between the big rock and our rock wall behind the fire pit. We will have a nice sitting area, and the smoke will go up and away."

"Let's get the bark, then we can cut some more boughs to sit on," said Joseph.

Zane returned to the dead Douglas fir that had already given them so much. Many of its branches had become firewood for their camp. Zane made his way along the fallen tree to where the last thirty feet hung out into space. From his position he saw the tree was about ten inches around and firmly wedged in the fork of another tree.

The tip of his tree was only about twelve feet from the forest floor. Carefully easing himself down to a spot under the leaning tree and hanging on with both his hands and legs, he backed his way up toward the tip, kicking off the small branches as he went. Where the tree was about five or six inches across, he let go with his legs and bounced a couple of times. The tree flexed with his weight, so he moved a few more feet up and bounced again.

The treetop snapped away, dropping Zane to the ground. It was a fine pole about twenty feet long. They placed it up against the boulder and then added smaller branches. They quickly constructed a roof across the fire wall. With the framework finished, they were ready to make it waterproof.

By the time Zane had laid the roof poles, the boys were ready with the slabs of bark. Layering their way up, the quickly placed roof was strong and reasonably watertight.

"If we didn't have this bark, this would be a whole lot harder," Zane said. "We would have to lay on triple layers of branches to give us this kind of protection."

"We had better set some more land traps. If this turns into a real storm, it would be nice to have a little more food."

"Where should we put them?" Joseph asked, expecting his father wouldn't want to set up again in the same meadow.

"I kind of like the place where we saw all those deer. I bet we could get a jackrabbit out of that area."

Joseph stood, ready to go.

"Would it be okay if I stayed here?" Ty asked.

"Sure, you could lay some branches down here and even take a nap if you wanted to. We won't be long."

"Okay," Ty said, looking up at his father with tired eyes.

"Let's set up a nice spot for Ty before we go, okay, Joseph?"

"Sure," Joseph said, pulling his knife and walking off to cut boughs.

After a short while the three of them had made a comfortable bed under the lean-to. Zane rolled up the coyote pelt and positioned it like a pillow. Ty smiled, stretched out, and pulled the raccoon over him like a blanket. Zane covered him with more branches. Ty fell asleep before Zane and Joseph were out of sight.

Jogging comfortably through the forest, Zane and Joseph traveled unnoticed toward their destination. They moved fast enough to make good time, yet slow enough to not overlook what was happening around them.

At one point, without breaking stride, Zane slipped his throwing stick from its pouch and hurled it at a gray squirrel hiding in the fork of a tree, not twenty feet from them. The stick slammed the tree to the left of the astonished squirrel. As the stick bounced past his head, the squirrel raced for the protection of the high branches.

Zane retrieved his stick and continued to the area where he

and Joseph intended to set their traps. They stopped at the tree line where the landscape changed from timber to brush. Standing inside the cover of branches, they watched the clearing. Not moving, not leaning, hardly blinking, they watched for signs of life. Evaluating the terrain, they decided where to place the snares. Keeping their heads below the top of the brush, they moved silently into the selected areas. Their pace was more fluid than slow, almost careless in practiced motion. A circuit of the area took about forty minutes and left eight traps.

Heading northwest, Zane and Joseph soon intersected the creek that fed their lake. They drank their fill and bathed as best they could in the shallow stream.

Relaxing on the bank and watching the sky now black with clouds, Zane retold the story of his great-grandfather and how he and many others went with Chief Joseph, and how the soldiers kept them from going into Canada. Zane told of the great bravery in battle, the cunning in their strategies, and the incredible strength of even the smallest child. Finally, he talked about the surrender and life at the reservation.

"Joseph, it is important that you remember this story as truly as you can, so you can tell it to your children. My grandfather told me many stories. You have heard most of them. Over the years, you will hear them all many times. It is our history; we are responsible for its telling. If we lose it, we will lose so much more than just stories."

The story had taken some time, and the sun was getting ready to drop behind the mountains.

"Let's go check our snares."

Zane and Joseph trotted swiftly to their traps. The air was sweet with moisture. It could start pouring at any moment. A quick check of the traps yielded nothing, so Zane and Joseph headed for camp. The rain started about a quarter of a mile before they arrived. It started slowly and built steadily. Even with the protection of the trees, Zane and Joseph were half soaked by the time they reached the cover of the lean-to.

Ty was sitting up, feeding the fire. "Did you guys get anything?" Ty asked.

"Nope, it is dried raccoon for dinner," Zane answered.

"I'll get it," Joseph said, bolting through the downpour to the entrance of the wickiup.

When Joseph returned, Zane had stripped to his breechclout. His clothes and boots were dried by the fire. He took the bundle of freshly tanned skins and tied each one onto the framework at the high point of the lean-to. Adding small green branches to the fire, smoke rolled thickly up to engulf the skins.

"They might smell us coming, but we won't smell like spoiled brains," Zane said with a smile.

The clouds kept the warmth of the day close to the earth. After plugging the few small roof leaks, branches were spread to minimize splash back. Zane and his boys settled into a peaceful evening. Their clothes dried despite the damp air. The skins cured in the rich smoke while Zane told his sons stories.

The telling lasted until late into the night. The rain pounded the bark roof to the rhythm of Zane's voice. Sometimes, he would speak the old language. Then he would repeat the words in English. The stories brought sadness, laughter, excitement, concern, and pride. When it finally came to an end, everyone was exhausted. Leaving a banked, smoldering fire, the three tired men crawled into a restful sleep.

In Zane's dream, a large, old, black bear walked into the camp and sat down under the lean-to. Warming its front paws at the fire, he turned his gray face toward the wickiup. He smiled an ominous warning as lightning flashed from his teeth. He clapped his bone-crushing paws together, and thunder filled the valley. Then, he stood and lumbered out of camp.

It was still raining the next morning when Zane awoke. He lay calmly for a while, listening to his sons sleeping and the rain pounding the top of the wickiup. Then a smile swelled across his face, but it was more than a smile, and his laughter filled the wickiup.

Like a dream come true, like a prophet visited by God, Zane understood.

The boys didn't know what to say, so they started laughing, too. After a couple of minutes, Zane turned to Ty and asked, "What is so funny?" For a moment they were all quiet, then they started to laugh again. They laughed until their hurting sides forced them to stop.

Lifting the door aside, they looked out into the pouring rain.

"This looks like a good day for staying around camp," Zane said, staring out the door.

"Yeah, a guy could get wet out there," Joseph agreed.

Zane took some of the meat, his bow stave, and his spear, and he light-footed it over to the lean-to. Joseph and Ty soon followed.

"We need to make arrows, arrow points, and quivers. What would you like to do first?" he asked his boys.

"Let's make arrowheads first, okay?" Ty asked Joseph.

"Anything sounds fine to me."

Zane took down the elk hide and cut off two four-inch-square pieces. Then he gave the elk antlers to the boys and told both to cut off a five- or six-inch piece from the tip.

"Don't chop with your knives. The steel of a knife is not made for chopping. That can snap a knife blade. Carve the antler through."

While the boys worked on the antlers, Zane went to work on the quivers. The pattern would be basic. He would make a tube about thirty-six inches long and seven to eight inches wide, tie the bottom two or three inches up, and then roll up to the tie and turn the tube inside out. Next, he would fold the top down about eight inches or so and cut fringe into the first six inches of the fold down. Then they would make a tube half the diameter of the first quiver and ten inches longer for the bow. After finishing the bow quiver the same as the arrow quiver, the two tubes would be lashed together. Last, he would add a shoulder strap.

With methodical patience, Zane started to cut out the quivers, the laces, and the straps. Joseph and Ty worked for hours, finally cutting through the antlers. Zane gave them lessons in holding the flint, what to look for in the point, and how to work with what the stone had to offer. This was not new for Joseph. He had heard it before, but he listened attentively, trying to glean something new.

After Zane showed them, he watched them work. Then he went back to preparing the parts for the quivers. Knowing that the boys would be occupied for most of the day, he resumed his own projects. Looking down the length of his spear, he imagined that the once mighty tree had grown this perfect branch so it could rest in his hands this day.

Zane cut three long narrow strips from the elk hide and laid them into the water to soak. Then he cut the weasel into two pieces slightly above the hind legs. Using a sharpened bone for an awl and some of the sinew for thread, Zane sewed the skin into place. The back half was fixed about eight inches from the blunt end of the spear, the head and body piece secured eight inches below the point. Next, he took the leather strips and stretched them tightly into place. Finally, he wrapped a high grip about ten inches long, as well as another below the balance point of the spear.

Although not intended to be decorative, it was a beautiful piece of work. He had dreamed of this spear once. Now, he proudly held it.

Joseph and Ty had each made four or five arrow points. Joseph's were more tailored than Ty's, but all were very serviceable small game points.

The rain had turned into a steady drizzle. The kind of weather that makes men feel trapped by the wet and the mud. Their dry comfortable work was a pleasant distraction amidst the cold splattering that surrounded them.

A cup of coffee would be nice, Zane thought as he showed his sons how to build their quivers.

After the boys became engrossed in their new project, Zane started fashioning the coyote fur into a cape. Small supple branches were sewn into the skin to help the head hold its shape. Straps held the front legs together across his chest. When finished, the cape lay comfortably over Zane's shoulders and down his back. He tied his hair back and used two sticks as if they were hat pins to hold the coyotes' head firmly over his own.

Past midday, Zane built a fire. They all put down their projects to eat and enjoy the warmth.

Ty washed out a couple of little cuts but didn't mention them.

If Dad could take that raccoon bite, then I can take these. But these obsidian cuts sting like fire, Ty thought.

After munching on dried raccoon, the boys were ready to resume their labors. This was the culmination of their previous week's work. Everything they had hunted and gathered was shaped into tools. Their excitement showed in their eyes. They were learning skills that other boys could only dream of. These were lessons they would remember for their entire lives. This was the real world.

Zane took down the raccoon pelt and fitted it to Ty's head, finishing it the same as he had the coyote. The raccoon face extended out like the brim of a hat above Ty's face. The body lay over his shoulders and back. The tail reached below his son's bottom.

"You look great," Zane said, pinning the headdress on Ty's hair.

"I wish I had a mirror." He grinned. "If mine looks as good as yours, then I really like it."

"They are the same," Joseph said. "You guys are awesome."

It was late afternoon, and the boys had their bows resting in the bow quivers. The last finishing touches were being applied to the arrow quivers.

SEVENTEEN

Zane took out his bow stave and followed the same procedure that he had given the boys. He removed the bark, cutting the length, finding the middle, and determining the bend. Then he started to shape his bow. The shape he chose was different from the continuous taper the boys had finished. He preferred a flat back with a slight cone-shaped bow. It was a little more complex and required more skill in uniform shaping, but it produced a stronger bow, and one that Zane felt was more pleasant to use.

He had made many bows over the years. He could never tell exactly what it would be like until he finished. It was a thrill to find what the wood had to offer. Zane worked the wood with love and kindness. Never rushing, he encouraged the bow to develop to its greatest potential using long gentle strokes.

Zane spent a lot of time with his boys. His work was always busiest when the boys had their free time from school, but he and Sara had decided that, if more time together during the summer meant less overtime money, it was a worthwhile trade-off. They never regretted their decision. Zane, Sara, and their sons were great friends, and he had always considered the pursuit of money in exchange for time with his family an unworthy trade.

These times were his favorite. They were away long enough that accomplishing the task at hand was not an option and exposed enough that they would need to rely on each other. After a week away from the comforts of home, when the struggle for food and warmth taxed physical and mental strength, a person's weaknesses began to surface. Joseph and Ty were still young, but if things turned bad and they experienced real trouble, there were no two people anywhere that Zane would rather have standing beside him.

Joseph added the finishing touches to his quiver. Testing the fit on his back, he bent over, stood tall and then jogged in place.

"I think this should work just fine," Joseph said as he placed the quiver on the ground next to him.

Joseph then sorted the arrow shafts that they had collected when looking for sticks for the fish traps. He had found eight, while Ty had found only three, but Joseph took half and gave the rest to Ty.

Ty's hands ached from working the stiff leather, but his new bow was finally finished. If he could complete the quiver and a couple of arrows, then maybe he could hunt this evening. He didn't dare stop for a minute. After finally getting the strap onto the quiver, he fitted it to his body. He bent forward, stood up straight, and reached over his shoulder for arrows. Deciding it was fine, he tied the strap securely into place. The fringe wasn't cut, but the quiver lay comfortably across his back.

I can cut the fringe later if I want, Ty thought.

"You guys take a break. Those quivers came out great," Zane said, laying his bow aside.

"Thanks, I can cut the fringe later. All we need now are arrows."

Joseph put his arrow shafts away. Taking up the last of the sinew, he started separating it into small strands, laying them neatly side by side.

"Do you guys want to take a break?" Zane asked.

"I'd kind of like to keep going, Dad. I want to shoot my bow," Ty explained, his face contorted with hope.

"Suit yourself. You can help Joseph prepare the sinew. Then you need to bark the arrow shafts. When you have done that, you make sure the full length of the shaft is smooth. Then you cut an angled nock into the end of the arrow. Don't cut it deep, just about one-quarter inch. After that, you wrap from the nock up about one-half inch. Then I'll show you how to break a notch into the fore shaft for your point."

"What are we going to do for feathers, Dad?" Joseph asked.

"The best feathers are from ravens or turkeys. But right now, we will work with what is available. I think we will have to trap a couple of those stellar jays in the meadow next to the lake."

Joseph nodded as he smiled, still working on the partially dried tendons. Ty sat beside his brother. Laying his quiver with his bow and arrow shafts on his lap, he went to work separating the sinew.

Zane took off his shirt, pants, and boots and then put on his breechclout, over-boots, and coyote cape, tying a leather strap from the head of the cape under his chin to hold it more securely against the wind.

"I'll be back in a couple of hours," Zane said, picking up his spear and stepping out into the drizzling rain.

The cold rain washed across him. The exertion of his run would keep the cold from penetrating beyond his skin. Cold had never been Zane's enemy. It did not lull him into complacency like the midsummer sun. It kept his senses sharp. The cold was a companion in the mountains like a dangerous friend. One couldn't take it for granted. One day, you might lie down and get too comfortable to get up. Then you would dream a dream of fools like the young cousin elk, who had been too young to be alone in his first late winter storm.

I thank you for your many gifts, little cousin. I hope one day you will walk again and grow to be a wise old man, Zane thought as he ran swiftly through the trees.

He gained the ridge where the boys had touched the deer two days earlier. Running with concentrated speed, he pressed against the falling rain.

An hour out of camp, he stopped on a rocky ledge that overlooked the eastern valleys. Standing silently in the misty rain, an endless view of ridges shrouded with clouds lay before him. The ocean of mist washed the trees and fed the low plants. The grasses fed the rabbits and deer, which fed the predators. All of these had given life to the Nez Perce people from the beginning of time. Zane stood still and gave honor to this circle of life that now gave life to his family.

My brothers have stood here before me. My sons will come after I am gone. For what would the world be like without the wolf, the grizzly bear, or the Nez Perce?

Zane stopped to check the snares on his way back to camp. He took a jackrabbit from one. The animal that had tripped the other one had chewed its way free from the leather. The rain washed away the tracks, but the teeth marks in the leather showed it to be a fox or a young coyote. If Zane had found it still in the trap, he would have set it free, unharmed. He had no need for the pelt, nor taste for the meat.

The coyote he had already taken would have eaten the rabbits and squirrels that he and his sons had consumed. They would leave this place as if they had never come. Zane thought about the predator that had freed itself, wondering if it could have been one of the little people who lived half in the spirit world and half in the physical world. Setting too many traps created a danger. It was not wise to anger the spirits. Soon they would have bows and would not need to trap anymore. It would be better.

When Zane arrived at camp, Joseph and Ty were not around. Their tracks led toward the lake, so Zane left his spear in camp and headed after them.

He found his sons sitting under the protective umbrella of a large fir near the edge of the lake. They had just dressed after taking their refreshing, but less than pleasant, bath.

Ty spotted his father at the same time Zane spotted him. When he was close enough to hear, Ty called out, "Hi, Dad! Did you get that rabbit with your spear?"

Zane trotted up to the tree before he answered. "He was in a snare. Will you skin and clean him? We will have him for dinner. I'm going to wash this mud off me."

"You bet," Joseph said, picking up the hare.

"I'll do it," Ty said, pulling his knife.

When his sons had finished, they returned to camp and put the hare on the spit over the fire. It was Joseph's turn to cook, so he sat closest to the fire. Feeding the fire sticks when needed, he maintained a consistent flame. The jack roasted to a deep golden brown. Cooked to perfection, it was ambrosia in their mouths, a meal worthy of savoring every bite.

While Joseph cooked, Zane showed the boys how to size their arrows. Then he showed them how to break a notch in the fore shaft of the arrow for the point.

Joseph and Ty had already notched and wrapped the nock ends. So, after they had broken a notch into the fore end of each arrow, they were ready for the points. Zane looked over the arrowheads the boys had made, and he did a little fine tuning to give them a little sharper edge and a bit more uniform size and weight. Then he showed the boys how to set and wrap them into the shafts.

Zane worked on his bow while Joseph and Ty put their arrows together. By the time they were ready for sleep, arrows rested comfortably in their quivers ready for feathers.

Eighteen

Zane awoke at his normal time, about an hour before light. As he opened the wickiup door, he could see, hear, and smell that the day would be warm and clear. Slipping out, he worked on his bow until the boys were ready to get up.

When they peeked out, the first daylight was casting shadows across their little clearing.

"You guys had better hurry down to the creek if you want to get any fish from our traps," Zane said.

Joseph and Ty slipped on their shoulder bags and their quivers, and they trotted across the still muddy ground. Wading the shallow creek, the boys successfully herded some nice brook trout into their traps. One was nearly twelve inches long. They cleaned and then wrapped the fish in a rabbit skin and stowed them in Joseph's shoulder bag. Then they strung their bows. Each knocking an arrow, they hunted their way toward the snares.

Steam rose from every tree, bush, and blade of grass. The sky was reclaiming the water that it had given the day before. Within an hour, Joseph and Ty had both stripped to the waist. They each took several practice shots, being sure of their backstop so as not to damage their points.

Ty's bow pulled a little hard for him, but after half a dozen shots, he started getting used to it. The pull was just right for Joseph. He had used a compound bow on last year's deer, but he had always enjoyed using traditional tackle. After a few shots, he was hitting as good as Ty. Joseph and Ty took over an hour to get to the area where they had their snares. A rabbit at ten to fifteen yards might well go home with them. Rabbit was the preferred food, but what they really wanted was a bird. Without feathers, the accuracy of their arrows would never be good beyond fifteen yards.

None of the snares had been tripped. Joseph and Ty moved two of them to places that had a greater concentration of tracks. At both of these, they set up rows of sticks designed to funnel the animals using those trails into the traps. Pleased with their work, Joseph and Ty headed south. Before long they met the creek that fed the top of their lake. Following it down through the meadow, the boys were caught up with the festive atmosphere of the spring day.

They walked fast, talked in full voice, and shot their bows casually at clumps of grass. A short distance beyond bow range, squirrels played in trees and gathered seeds from the steamy ground. Birds fluttered, singing songs to the sunshine. The meadow was happy to be alive after forty hours of rain.

When the boys passed through the part of the meadow where they had seen the wolves, they slowed their pace and lowered their voices. The inhabitants of the meadow continued as if they had no memory of that day. Joseph and Ty remembered. The experience had affected each of them differently, but neither would ever forget that moment.

Zane sat on the top of the granite boulder, gathering warmth from the morning sun. Having finished the first half of his bow, he brushed the wood shavings away and examined the second half. Visualizing the bow limb that lay hidden within, Zane started again, sending long curls of wood rolling across his legs.

Joseph and Ty crept back up to their clearing. Spotting their father on top of the rock, they circled around behind him then slipped in close behind the stone wall. With wide grins, they popped up, "Hi, Dad. What...?"

Stopping mid-sentence, the boys looked up at the space their father had occupied.

"You boys have a nice walk?" Zane asked.

Joseph and Ty nearly jumped out of their boots.

"Yaa!" Ty screamed, turning around, then covered his mouth and laughed.

Zane stood behind them, holding his half-finished bow.

Joseph started laughing, too. "Did you hear us?" he asked.

"Did you get any fish?" Zane asked, avoiding the question.

"We sure did," Ty answered, "and our bows shoot great."

"Let's have something to eat. Then maybe you can get some feathers for your arrows."

Joseph and Ty unstrung their bows and leaned them against the wickiup. Zane sat down and started again on his bow while the boys built a fire and roasted the midmorning breakfast.

"We need to gather the traps tonight," Zane began, still giving concentrated attention to his bow. "Tomorrow morning, we are going to break down this camp. The sweat lodge is about an hour and a half past the fish traps. We can stay there tomorrow and then start our walk out the day after."

"Do we have to go?" Ty asked with a sorrowful voice.

"It is five or six days out." Zane said, putting his hand on Ty's back. "Our trip isn't over yet."

After eating the tasty morsels of fish, Zane returned to his labors atop the granite boulder. Joseph and Ty went out to the meadow next to the lake. They gathered six fir boughs and loosely wove them together in twos. Then they took them to a small cluster of trees that stood in the meadow at the edge of the lake. Ty watched Joseph set the delicate deadfall triggers under them.

"Why don't we use something heavy for the trap? Won't they wiggle out from under these?" Ty asked.

"We don't want to kill the birds. We only want a couple of feathers."

"It's okay. I would eat it," Ty insisted.

"No sense in killing it if we don't have to," Joseph answered.

"Did Dad teach you how to make these?"

"Last year when Tom, Dad, and I went hunting deer in Utah, we used a trap like this to catch a little songbird. Tom pulled one of its feathers and tied it to my bow. It was a big joke for him, but Dad was really serious. I think I was making too much noise or something."

Tom had been Zane's best friend since they were children. When Zane's grandfather was alive, Zane and Tom would sit and listen for hours to his stories. Now when they were together, they would speak in the old language.

Tom wasn't huge as far as men go, but he was large for a Nez Perce. He was six-foot-two-inches tall and two-hundred-twenty pounds of muscle. He could run almost as fast as Zane, and he could shoot a hunting bow as well as any man. Ty figured Tom was probably the only man alive who might be able to whip his dad. He knew that would never happen, though. In thirty years, they had never spoken a cross word to one another. They would walk into hell for each other.

Ty and Tom were good friends, too. They had the same determined focus in life. They were kindred spirits. This year, the four of them planned to go elk hunting in Wyoming. Ty couldn't wait.

Joseph finished setting the triggers under the traps. Next, the boys pulled and raked with their hands all the fir and spruce needles and ground covering from under and around the traps. Then, they scratched the moist earth with sticks, all the time being loud and generally attracting attention to themselves. When they were finished, they washed their hands in the crystal blue lake, had a long cold drink, and returned to camp.

Jays were the first to swoop in onto the freshly dug earth, hopping around to gobble up the insects the boys had uncovered. Then the little snowbirds, still in their winter white and black, started landing onto the lower branches. A group of six or seven danced around, fluttering away then back again, giving ground to the larger more aggressive jays.

A gray camp robber sat on a branch above the action. As big as the jays and just as bullish, he screamed down at the other birds. The snowbirds covered the ground as quickly as they could. The jays paid little attention but screamed back.

The robber dropped down, scattering the small birds. Bounding twice, he snapped up a beetle desperately racing for cover. With its treat in its beak, the fat bird hopped to a low branch to swallow the snack. Screaming, the branch fell away, and the boughs blanketed the birds' reaching wings. The beetle scurried to safety while its captor lay pinned. With terrified eyes staring into the green needles, the bird lay motionless, pressed to the earth, anxiously awaiting its fate.

The other birds bolted to the nearby branches. Looking and listening, they could see no real change. The bully was gone, and they were glad to be rid of him. After a tense moment, they returned to their lunch.

Zane still sat on the rock, working the bow limb. The second side was starting to show good shape. He could feel the strength and grace that the bow would soon have. He felt the spirit of the tree guiding his hands. The tree had grown in another time. It had learned the lessons of life from a different world. Then when life had almost been taken from it, Zane came. Taking this small part, Zane offered the tree life once again. There were four hundred years of knowledge within its fibers. When Zane loosed an arrow, a power much greater than his would send it forth.

Joseph and Ty wandered back into the camp. Plopping down onto the sunbaked rocks, Joseph lay back, stretching out to gather in rays. Ty sat sullenly, pitching small rocks at an unknown target.

"What do you want to do?" Ty asked Joseph.

"I want to kick back for about an hour or so. Then we could see if we have any feathers for our arrows."

"I don't want to hang around. I'm going for a walk."

"Where do you think you will be going?" Zane asked, looking at his younger son.

"I think I'll head over to the ridge where we saw that doe."

Zane thought for a moment. "If you go up that ridge, stay out of the valley to the east. You know your way pretty well, but I don't want you taking any chances."

"Dad, I won't get lost," Ty protested as he put on his quiver and shoulder bag.

Ty strode out of the camp with an air of confidence. When he looked back, his dad was giving full attention to his bow. Joseph looked like he was asleep.

I won't get lost, Ty thought as he headed off into the timber.

NINETEEN

Ty had hunted alone a few times. Always in places where Dad, Joseph, Tom, and he had been before or in basin areas or valleys closely surrounded by roads. This was the first time he was out alone in a place with complicated ridge lines and valleys going in different directions.

Ty's bold pace slowed to a casual walk. After twenty minutes, he still felt pretty sure he was heading in the right direction. It was hard to see landmarks in low rolling areas covered with tall timber. Ty realized he hadn't paid very good attention to things when he and Joseph had walked around. Half an hour later Ty felt a little scared and wondered if he should head west to the lake. At least that way he could follow it around to the creek, then up onto the ridge.

Up ahead it looked like the trees opened a little. Ty broke into a trot. Maybe he would be able to see where he was. From trepidation to clarity, he walked right out of the trees onto the edge of the meadow. After looking about for a moment, he realized that he was standing in the same spot where he had first seen this meadow.

I knew it, Ty thought. *It's just a little way in that direction, and up the ridge.*

Walking briskly now, he soon began to head uphill. Nearing the place where he and Joseph had seen the doe, Ty shifted into a hunting mode. Walking slowly up the game trail, arrow ready, Ty strained his senses. The midday sun pulled drops of sweat from his forehead. They rolled down into his eyes.

He wiped his face with the back of his hand then remembered his dad telling him, "Wiping your face with your hand is like waving hello to everything around you. It has to be done carefully, if you don't want to be seen."

But it bugs me! Ty thought as he scrubbed the sweat off his face with his jacket. Then he quickly looked around to see if his father was watching him.

"I don't see any animals walking around anyway," Ty said aloud.

He ambled up the trail, his bow hanging in his left hand. The higher he pressed the ridge, the greater the panoramic view of the valley behind him opened up into its primeval perfection. Looking back, he could, for the first time, really see the ridges to the west of their lake. They reached up with rugged perfection until they formed a series of snow covered peaks that half framed the valley.

This is so beautiful. I wish mom could see this, Ty thought as he continued on his way. He didn't know how far he had gone, but it was a long way. The valley to the east continued to widen the higher he climbed. He moved from one place to another, trying to find a clear view of the valley floor, but the tree line on the ridge limited him to glimpses of what lay beyond.

Finally, Ty scrambled up onto a large rock, not so much to rest but to think about what to do. *I should probably head back,* he thought as he looked out over the acres of brush that lay like a clearing down to the west side of the ridge. After a couple of minutes, he decided he would go a bit farther up the ridge. Ty turned onto his belly, slipped over the edge of the rock and dropped to the ground.

When he hit the ground, two large mule deer bucks stood

straight up, not thirty feet in front of him. They looked at Ty's open mouth and bounded away. As they went, three smaller bucks jumped up and trotted off in a different direction. Ty slipped an arrow from his quiver, but they were long gone.

Disgusted with himself for not having seen so many deer right at his feet, he kept repeating, "I can't believe it." He walked about thirty feet, cursing and kicking the ground. Then the thunder of wings beat the air. A dozen mountain grouse broke from cover right at his feet. Ty jumped, almost falling backward. The grouse flew to the ridge, set their wings, and glided over the east side.

Ty reached his arrow to his string at a dead run, trying to keep the birds in sight. As they glided over the rise, he could only see the direction that they were headed. He forced himself to go slowly over the ridge.

Mountain grouse weren't very smart if they hadn't been hunted. Ty had never gotten one before, but his dad brought some home every year. He struggled to remember what he had been told about hunting grouse. He did remember his father saying if you were slow and quiet, sometimes you can walk right up to them. If only he had looked around better when he was sitting on the rock, he'd have gotten a clean shot.

Ty moved forward, wanting to hurry to find them but trying desperately to move slowly. Then he heard the cooing of their feeding calls, like dripping water from up ahead. He hunted forward, jittery with excitement. He hadn't felt like this since he had shot his deer the season before. Then he saw them about thirty yards ahead. Walking and looking back, not quite feeding any longer, they were on to him.

When they went into the brush, Ty hurried to close the gap. When he reached the edge of the brush, he saw the last two birds getting ready to disappear into the next cluster of bushes. He drew back and shot. The arrow brushed across the breast of the lead bird. Startled, it fell backward and rolled. Gaining its footing, it rocketed into the air. Followed by the rest of the covey, it disappeared into the eastern valley. Ty ran over to where the bird had rolled.

"I hit him. Man, I know I hit him."

Ty found his arrow and examined it for blood. Finding it clean, he looked at the ground. No blood, but when it had taken off, it had lost three good size feathers. He looked around and found one more. Placing them carefully into his shoulder bag, he walked over to where the grouse had made their final exit. It was a rocky point standing over a cliff-like edge. Stretching out before him was an ocean of valleys and ridges covered in timber. Meadows dotted the landscape.

This is where I want to live, Ty thought, looking out at the wilderness paradise. *I have to tell Dad about this place.*

Ty walked back, feeling like he had finally come of age. Being out alone didn't scare him now. He could make a fire, and he could set a trap. He didn't get lost. And next time he would hunt smart, like his father always said. Next time, he could get one of those deer.

"I just wish I'd seen those grouse when I was up on that rock."

Joseph sat up and then bent forward, stretching the knots out of his back. He looked up at his father, who was in even tempo, sending curl after curl of wood rolling off his bow like a craftsman plying his trade.

Joseph put on his quiver and walked out to check his bird traps. As he got close, his heart jumped. Two traps were down. When he reached the traps, he knelt and shook them. The last thing he wanted to do was reach under and find a rattlesnake. You don't normally find snakes this high up or this early, but he wasn't going to be foolish.

Joseph raised an edge of the bough trap, lifting it slowly so as not to release any pinned birds. Then he saw the tail of a little snowbird. Joseph continued to lift the branches carefully until he was sure that was the only prisoner.

"Are you okay, little guy?" Joseph said, gently picking up the bird. Holding the tiny bird in his hand, Joseph gently stroked its back until it calmed down from its shock.

"Your feathers won't help me, little guy. You better see if you can find your buddies." Joseph held his palm out flat. The bird gave one last terrified look to Joseph and flashed into the air. It landed on a nearby branch, looked around, and then hurried off to find its friends.

Joseph repeated the procedure on the second trap. This time he picked up the much more aggressive camp robber. "You are a fat boy," said a smiling Joseph as he held the bird in his hand. "I hope this doesn't hurt too much."

The bird resisted. Joseph was as gentle as he could be, but when it was over, he had two feathers from each wing and one tail feather. Feeling totally abused, the bird flew to the nearest high branch and screamed avian obscenities at Joseph. Even when he was on the other side of the meadow, he could hear the bird complaining to the world about Joseph's outrageous behavior.

"I don't think he likes me," Joseph said to himself as he disappeared into the trees.

Zane showed Joseph how to split the quill into vanes. Then how to wrap the vane high on the shaft as if it were upside down and going toward the point, folding it back over the wrap so it rested in the right place. Then how to take up the wrap next to the nock and rewrap it, so it would hold down the vane as well as reinforce the nock. Then how to lay the vane across a piece of wood and crop the feathers to an even edge.

"Two vanes on each arrow straight back from the point edges will work fine," Zane said while adding the finishing touches to the feathers.

"That looks great," Joseph said, admiring their work.

"Make sure you measure your starting place right so your nock wrapping will hold the back of the vane. And be sure your feather is going back in the right direction after you fold it over. If you have any questions, you know where to find me."

Joseph smiled at his dad. "Ty's been gone a long time."

"I thought he would be back by now, too, but he will be all right."

Joseph went to work on his arrows. Zane looked out at the trees then up at the sun before starting back into shaping his bow.

Ty walked back into camp with a wide grin on his face. "Don't you guys ever take a break?"

Joseph and Zane put down their tools, happy to see Ty back.

"Where did you go?" Joseph asked.

"I went up that ridge like I said. I bet I hiked nearly ten miles. I saw five bucks, and I shot a grouse. But it got away."

"You shot a grouse?" Joseph said excitedly. "Do you think we could go back and find them?"

"No way. They are gone. They flew over this cliff and down into a deep valley. We could never find them. The one I shot I hit in the breast. It rolled over and knocked the arrow out. Then it flew away. It was incredible. When it was flapping around, these came out." Ty produced the four feathers from his bag. "You should have been there."

"These are awesome," Joseph said, looking at the feathers. "We got two birds in our traps. One was too little, but the other one was a big gray jay. I got five feathers out of him. You should have heard him screaming at me after I let him go. He didn't like it at all."

"I bet he liked it better than being eaten," Ty added with a smile.

"I don't know. We could ask him. I bet he is still up in that tree screaming at me."

Both boys laughed. Joseph was glad that Ty was all right, and Ty wished he could see that jay tomorrow still sitting in the tree and screaming about getting its feathers pulled.

Joseph showed Ty how to fit the feathers to the arrows. The grouse feathers were larger than the jays, so the boys divided them equally. Ty told about his walk while they worked on their equipment.

After a couple of hours, they admired their quivers of arrows. Now they were ready for anything.

"Dad, I'm getting hungry."

"I am, too, Ty. I want to save the rest of the dried meat. We only have two days' supply left. We had better go hunting."

"Dad, I'm tired. I've been walking all day," Ty protested.

"You can hunt the trees near the lake. They are loaded with squirrels. Walk slow and quiet until you find a good group. Then sit down in some cover and wait. You will get a shot. Joseph and I will work a wide circle around the snares. We will probably be back shortly after dark. Go ahead and cook it up if you get one before we return."

Ty was too tired to go for another long walk, but the squirrel idea sounded good. A roasted gray squirrel would be just right.

Joseph strung his bow, and Zane put his throwing stick in its pouch and took up his spear. "Good hunting, Ty," Zane and Joseph each said as they trotted out of camp.

Ty was anxious to try out his new arrows. He also wanted to get his first kill with his new bow. He strolled down to the lake. After taking a long drink, he took off his boots and dangled his feet in the crisp, refreshing water. Lying back into the damp grass, Ty chewed on a long stem and gazed sleepily out into the blue sky. Then his head perked up as he strained to the sound. Behind him in the trees he could hear the raucous chatter of gray squirrels. His father had been right. After putting on his boots and gathering his equipment, Ty crept cautiously into the forest canopy.

Twenty

Zane and Joseph moved with casual precision, slipping along at a slow fluid pace like cats on a prowl. Joseph watched his father trotting before him.

He never trips, and he never gets tired, Joseph thought. *What do you see? What do you hear? What does great grandfather tell you as you run through these woods?* His own thoughts startled him. *Do I really believe Dad can hear great grandfather?*

"The way that Dad and Mom see things is so different. They both tell me that I will be a great man one day. The trouble is they seem to have opposite plans for me. I just wish Mom would come out here with us. Things have a way of becoming clear out here in the mountains."

He returned his attention to what was happening around him, just in time to miss running into his father as Zane made a U-turn in front of him. Not knowing if his father had seen an animal to shoot or not, Joseph stopped as quietly as he could and watched for a signal as to what to do next.

Zane took a couple of steps back then sat down cross-legged, facing a small tangle of bushes. He placed his spear beside him and put his hands on his knees. Joseph, not knowing what to do, sat down about three feet away from his father. Looking at his father's face, he knew he shouldn't speak, but he sure wished he knew what was going on.

After a couple of minutes of silence, Joseph heard a crash in the bushes his father was facing. It sounded like something was tearing them apart. When the disturbance started, Zane began speaking Nez Perce in a calm soothing voice. Joseph was surprised how much he could understand. He still didn't speak the language very well, but being around Dad and Tom, he had become able to understand the essence of the words spoken in his presence.

"How are you, my little cousin?" Zane began. "I had hoped I could find you. With your knowledge and your wisdom, you walk this forest unmolested. You know more about this place than I will ever know. There is a wise old warrior that walks with the spirit of a black bear. More bears have fallen to your spears than will ever fall to the spears of man. Tell me, my little cousin, if this bear is my enemy, where do I strike? Tell me, my little friend, and I and my sons and their sons will sing of your wisdom."

The fat, old porcupine stepped from the brush toward the murmuring sound of Zane's voice. As he stepped into the open, not six feet from Zane and Joseph, Zane's voice fell silent. The porcupine rose onto his hind legs and tested the air with his nose. The changing breeze gave Zane and Joseph away. The porcupine dropped to his feet, lowered his head, and flared his forest of deadly spines. Spinning in place, he whipped his tail, and a few errant quills pierced the low branches as he exited back into his bushy sanctuary.

Zane sat for a moment, and then he gathered the half dozen quills that had been left behind. He wrapped them in a length of leather and stowed them in his shoulder bag.

They continued their hunt in silence. Fifteen minutes later, they slipped carefully into a shallow wash. Occasionally creeping up and peering into the adjacent hollows, they worked their way along looking for game.

After a while Zane and Joseph were looking at a small clearing while lying on the edge of their hidden path. When Joseph was satisfied that there were no animals visible, he started to back off so he could proceed down the small gully. Zane put his hand on Joseph's shoulder and pointed to a clump of tall grass tucked into some brush at the edge of the clearing.

Joseph looked hard, then spotted a flick of movement. After straining to determine what he was seeing, it was as if his eyes came into focus and the head of a mule deer appeared in the grass. It had been there all the time, perfectly camouflaged, lying in the grass and chewing an afternoon snack.

As they watched the deer, a cottontail rabbit hopped out into the clearing. Then another appeared on the edge, not twenty feet from where they lay hidden. Joseph drew back an arrow and let it fly. The rabbit was hit squarely. It rolled once and died kicking in the grass.

The mule deer's head perked up at the sound. Next to it another deer head popped up. The second rabbit ran to the edge of the clearing and froze, looking at his fallen friend. Joseph drew back another arrow and sent it after his second victim. It struck the rabbit in the back leg. It spun around and started to run as best as it could.

The deer and Zane all sprang to their feet at the same time. The deer spun to run as Zane hurled his spear. The seven-foot dart flew straight, striking the rabbit mortally to the ground. Joseph grinned at his father.

"When you threw, I thought you were going for that big doe that was closest to us. I can't believe how fast you got that spear into the air. You could have got that deer."

Zane grinned back at his son as they walked over to the first rabbit that Joseph had hit.

"I probably could have. They were pretty lucky you weren't hunting deer, too."

Zane picked up the rabbit and pulled the arrow that had pierced both lungs and the heart.

"Perfect shot."

"Thank you, gentle cousin, for your gift of meat."

Joseph took the rabbit and the arrow.

"Boy, I hit him square, didn't I? I wish I would have hit the other one better."

"They were both great shots. I only know a handful of men that have gotten two rabbits in one day with a bow they made in the mountains." Zane handed Joseph the second rabbit then carefully cleaned off his spear.

Zane and Joseph field-dressed the two rabbits then tied them to Joseph's shoulder bag.

"Dad," Joseph asked as they looked in the direction of their traps, "what did you learn from the porcupine?"

"What did you learn, Joseph?"

Joseph stopped walking and looked at his father. "Dad, I learned that I have a lot more to learn."

Zane smiled. "That's what I learned, too, son."

Both smiled and continued on, each fading into his own thoughts.

When Zane and Joseph picked up the snares, one was tripped but empty.

"Nice job on these," Zane said as he dispersed any sign of the traps. "You and Ty have done a great job on this trip. You are ready to do this alone."

Zane thought for a moment, then added, "When that time comes and you are out alone, remember, it seldom goes this easy. Sometimes you have to work harder and smarter, but you'll be okay. Soon you will find a strength that only a handful of men now have. That day you will be a Nez Perce warrior. From that time a thousand braves will stand beside you wherever you go. Hunyawat will give you a Wyakin, a protecting and guiding spirit. Your Wyakin is a private part of you. From that time, you will lose your childhood fears. You will be a great man among our people."

The sun was setting as Zane and Joseph were walking back to camp. The birds sang their last chorus of the day, and the evening chill began to sweep across the landscape. A squirrel took one last look around before disappearing into its tree-top nest, thankful for the last moment of another glorious day.

"Do you miss anything when we come on these trips?" Joseph asked.

"I miss your mother, and I miss hot coffee and hot showers and clean teeth. But mostly, I miss your mother."

Zane and Joseph both laughed.

"Me, too," Joseph agreed.

TWENTY-ONE

When Zane and Joseph arrived at camp, Ty was reclining with his feet up as he roasted a fat gray squirrel.

"How did you guys do?" Ty asked, eager to tell his own story.

"We got two rabbits," Joseph said in a casual voice.

"What is that you're cooking Ty?" Zane asked.

"Oh, just a gray squirrel," Ty said. "I got back into some brush like you said, and three of them came down to right in front of me. I nailed this one. He tried to get away with my arrow, and I hit him again. My bow shoots great. I'm going to use it for my deer this year."

"You guys have done a great job on your equipment," their father said. "You both should be very proud of yourselves. Let's go cook up these rabbits. We'll eat one tonight and save the other for later."

After dinner, Zane resumed work on his bow. The second side was nearly finished. In another five hours or so, it would be ready for a string.

Zane and his sons were up before dawn, dismantling their camp. By the time the first squirrels warmed themselves in the early sun, there was little sign of human habitation. Soon, there would be no evidence of their passing, and the ebb and flow of life in the valley would remain as it had been for centuries. The valley lived in life's perfect balance of struggle and survival.

Zane wore his coyote cape and put his throwing stick in its pouch. He had tied his bow to the strap of his shoulder bag. His spear was cradled comfortably in his right hand.

Joseph had his quiver with bow and arrows on his back. On his shoulder bag, he tied the bundle of furs they had gathered from their trip.

Ty wore his raccoon cape, his bow and arrows in their quivers on his back, and his shoulder bag comfortably at his side.

The three men were well fed, rested, and prepared for the next part of their journey. They walked briskly to the fish traps. There were two nice brook trout trapped within, which they released before they dismantled and dispersed the traps.

Ty asked, "Why did you let the fish go?"

"We will fast today. The sweat lodge is about four miles from here. We will spend the day there, then start out tomorrow."

"How many days will it take to walk out?" Joseph asked.

"Whatever it takes," Zane answered.

Joseph and Ty smiled. They liked that kind of answer. Anything goes. Maybe they could even stretch it into another ten days.

Walking not hunting, they covered the four miles in quick time. The last quarter mile took them down a steep canyon to a small creek. There was a small, mostly flat grassy area with a small wickiup surrounded by thick willows and dense brush land downed trees. Joseph and Ty were obviously disappointed. They had expected something more than this tiny wickiup and a shallow creek. Their old camp had been a lot more cheerful than this damp, shaded canyon.

Zane started the fire while the boys gathered wood. While the rocks heated in the fire, they repaired and cleaned up the sweat lodge.

"We have a long way to go in these next several days. Today, we will prepare for what we might find along the way. This is not a day for joking or playing. Be as serious in your prayers as your mother expects you to be in church. Within the spirit world, you can find harmony or cold earth. It is your choice. Hunyawat, the one above all, knows when you are no longer children. Then he will reach out to you as men. You can be men with great power, or you can be just men. It is a privilege to have the choice."

Joseph listened to his father with respect.

Neither Ty nor Joseph felt much like a man. Joseph felt halfway between a boy and a man. Ty didn't like even thinking about it.

Ty felt tough enough to be a man, but if it meant doing too much alone without Joseph, he would rather wait a couple of years. The idea of overseeing more than himself and having grave responsibilities scared him. He still liked the idea that, if everything went wrong, Joseph or Dad would be there to take care of him.

All three stripped to breech clouts and brushed their bodies with sage and cedar before entering the sweat lodge. There was only enough room for them to sit cross-legged, facing each other, with the rock pit in the middle. Zane sat farthest in on the west side of the lodge, with Joseph and Ty on each side of the east facing door. When they were settled and the door was closed, it was dark with a wash of light finding its way between loose fitting bark slabs and pooling into corners of the small room.

Joseph and Ty waited for a moment, then heard a bubbling hiss as Zane poured some water onto the rocks. The thick steam rolled into the air with a smell of sage. As it rose up to the boys' faces, they let out comforting sighs as the moist aromatic cloud filled the small enclosure. While the steam circled them like a blanket, Zane started to sing an old song that they had heard before. They could not understand all the words, but it told of grace and balance in the world. It was a soft melody that reminded them of something from their past that was in the shadows of their memories.

As time went on, Zane poured water on the other side of the rock pit, and the steam filled the room once again. He talked about his love for his wife and his love for his sons. The three took turns praying for anything that was on their hearts, and they sang a song of thanksgiving together. After a while Zane pushed open the door, trotted over to the small pool and slipped in. Joseph and Ty followed him, taking the plunge. It took a moment for the cold to soak into their skin. When it did, a refreshing charge flashed across their bodies. After stoking the fire and switching out the rocks, they returned to the warmth of the sweat lodge.

Back inside the lodge, Zane spoke to his sons about how they were tied to their ancestral land and traditions. He explained that they would need to learn to navigate between the white road and the road of their ancestors. Zane sang, and they prayed. And after a while, they slipped out for another plunge into the icy water.

The third time in the lodge, Zane spoke of the times he had spent with his grandfather and how things had changed for their people, and he shared the pride and privilege The People felt before they were penned up like animals and forced from their old ways. They prayed for the preservation of the bear kingdom and the spirits that lived there. They also prayed for wisdom and strength and patience, as well as the resurrection of the tribe. Zane sang additional songs, and they sat silently in the steam-filled room.

During the fourth round in the sweat lodge, Zane talked about how the men of their tribe stood in the gap. He prayed for himself and for help to find his way in the world, and he expressed how it was a privilege for him to stand for his sons and those around him. His sons felt the pride and the strength that filled the room. They were fed by it. Then they prayed with their father, and all of their people who had come before them, the three singing together in the warm mist.

After the fourth round, they were finished. They dried themselves and dressed in their warm clothes.

Zane turned to Ty. "I'd like you to go out and hunt. Joseph and I are going to find places to sit and pray."

"Shouldn't I pray, too?" Ty didn't really want to. He really wanted to go hunting and get something to eat, but he didn't like being treated younger than Joseph.

"If you want to talk to me about it, ask me tomorrow. If you have time, why don't you cut some boughs for sleeping? We'll sleep over there."

Ty left camp with his equipment plus the snare cords. Trying to look upset, he was secretly thrilled to not have to sit for the rest of the day.

Zane and Joseph went off in different directions to find places of solitude. About a half hour before dark, Joseph walked back into camp. Ty was already there, feeding a warm and welcoming fire.

"How did it go?" Joseph asked.

"I did all right. I got two chipmunks, and I found some Miner's lettuce. I set some traps, but I didn't get anything yet. Do you know where Dad is?"

"Nope, I haven't seen him since this afternoon."

Zane strode into camp just at dark. "Hi, guys. Did you find something to eat, Ty?"

"Yep, a nice salad and two little squirrels."

"You are quite a hunter, Ty. Have you guys given any thought to sleeping?"

"I'm sorry, Dad. I forgot to cut branches."

"It will only take a few minutes if we work together," Zane said.

Zane dismantled the sweat lodge. He started with the support poles and broke them in half, then took the three-foot-long sticks and used a rock to drive them into the ground in two parallel lines about six inches apart and six feet from the fire. Then he used the boughs from the sweat lodge to fill the space between the two rows of sticks.

Joseph and Ty brought fir and pine boughs, piling them on the fire side of Zane's wall. Their father built another similar wall at a ninety-degree angle to the first one. The two-foot-high walls wrapped nearly halfway around the fire. Zane then added a few good-sized pieces of wood to the fire, covering it with about a half inch of dirt so that errant sparks would not light the forest.

"We have a big day tomorrow. Let's get some rest."

Zane and his sons made a comfortable nest in the fragrant branches. The warmth from the coals radiated over them like a soft blanket.

Zane experienced a fitful night. Like a warrior on the eve of battle, he felt his fate lay close at hand. No one can know their future. Life brings what it brings. If one is strong, they live and die with honor. With no regrets, a warrior charges the line.

"Come on, guys, it's time to get up."

Joseph and Ty sat up into the cold morning air. Rubbing the sleep out of their eyes, they stretched their bodies on the heels of a night spent atop a lumpy mattress, greeting the early morning with the innocence of youth.

"Ty, do you have traps out?" Zane asked his sleepy son.

"Yeah."

"How far away are they, and in which direction?"

Ty thought for a moment, knowing his father wanted an accurate answer. "There are two snares and two deadfalls a half mile or less, that way."

"Let's go ahead and break this camp down. We'll pick up your traps on the way."

Zane and his sons dispersed the pine and fir boughs as well as the fire ring and all other evidence of the camp. Zane gave each of the boys a piece of the cooked meat from his bag and then ate one himself.

"Let's go see how you did, Ty," Zane said with pride for his young son.

Ty and Joseph led the way out of camp with their bows strung. Zane followed closely, his spear cradled comfortably in his right hand. A short way down the creek, Ty found his traps. Two of them were sprung, but empty. After picking up the triggers, they headed northeast on a steady climb, diagonally up the side of the ridge.

Twenty-Two

Patchy clouds filled the sky, hurrying off to find a place to drop their precious burden. The morning slowly warmed into a pleasant day. Cloudy enough to give shade without feeling like a downpour was imminent. Within a couple of hours, Zane and his sons gained the ridge, which continued up to the north toward a snow-covered mountain. Looking below them to the east there was a wide valley spotted with meadows. Beyond this untouched wilderness garden were similar mountains and valleys far beyond the limits of their vision.

"Where are we going, Dad?" Joseph asked.

"About seventy miles that way," Zane said, pointing northeast. "If you guys needed to find your own way out of here, you could head due east, in the direction of the morning sun. You would reach the highway in about four days."

Joseph looked at his father and shuddered. "Maybe we should go that way, Dad," Joseph said with tears in his eyes.

Ty looked at Joseph like he was crazy. "Why? Dad, I'm not ready to head out yet! Joseph, why do you want to head out?"

"I don't know. I thought maybe we should, that's all," Joseph said. He knew that there was something his father was not voicing. Something that waited for him, which would challenge him beyond anything that he had ever experienced before. He feared for his father and for the change coming to his life, whatever the outcome.

"Well, I don't think we should," Ty added, feeling like Joseph had betrayed him.

"Life finds you wherever you are, Joseph. We could go to the closest road, but I'd rather walk than hitchhike, and we eventually have to get to our truck."

"Yeah, Joe, I can't believe you want to bail."

Joseph looked over at Ty. Ty didn't get it. Joseph hadn't told him his vision. *Even if he had, Ty probably wouldn't believe it,* Joseph thought.

"You're right, Ty. It was a stupid idea. I'd rather go out the regular way, too."

"Yeah!" Ty yelled. Suddenly everything was okay. Ty felt huge relief. They were all thinking the same again.

"Are we going straight across then?" Ty asked, pointing to the northeast.

"Head straight for the saddle; just north of the big peak."

"Okay, let's go." Ty led out. A young man full of confidence, eager for a new adventure, led the way forward. This was the best trip Ty had ever been on. Now he knew what it was like to trap, hunt and live in the most beautiful place on earth.

When I get older, I'm going to move out here. I could live in a tepee and go hunting every day. I can't believe Joseph wanted to bail, Ty thought as he led a quick pace down into the valley.

As Ty hurried off down the side of the ridge, Zane looked at his older son. "It's a beautiful day, isn't it, son?"

Joseph looked up and around, not wanting his father to see the tears in his eyes. "Yeah, Dad, it sure is." *It is truly a beautiful day,* he thought.

Zane placed his hand on his son's shoulder, then they both trotted downhill to catch up with Ty.

Water was plentiful this time of year. They crossed a creek or came upon a spring every couple of miles. They occasionally jumped-up deer. The deer were as curious as they were scared, moving clear but not bolting and heading for the next county.

After a while, Joseph said, "Boy, people don't get in here very often, do they?" A small buck trotted off to about sixty yards then stopped to watch the three pass.

"Not very often," Zane answered.

By noon the three black-haired leather clad travelers had made the ridge at the far end of their valley and had dropped down into the valley beyond. As they were going, they ate whatever edible plants they could find. It wasn't satisfying, but it was reasonably nutritious.

Zane killed a young squirrel with his throwing stick. The boys took a couple of shots with their bows but only managed to lose an arrow.

"You guys ready for a piece of meat?" Zane asked as they approached a fast-moving stream.

"Sounds good to me," Ty said, plopping down onto a large flat rock. "How far have we gone?"

"How far do you think, Joseph?" Zane said, shifting the question.

"I don't know, maybe eight or nine miles."

"That is a pretty good guess. We've made good time."

"No wonder I'm tired," Ty said.

"We're not in any big hurry to get out. The next nice place we see, we should set up camp."

Joseph and Ty ate what their father offered. The feeling of hunger relaxed within them. After a few minutes' rest and a long drink, the three were off again.

The boys' bows were unstrung and in their quivers. It was tiring carrying them at the ready all the time when they weren't really hunting. Besides, it would only take a moment to string it if they wanted to take a shot.

It had been a slow pace for Zane. If he was alone and he had a mind to, he could cover the seventy miles in two days. But Joseph and Ty were not yet able to cover that much ground. And like he had said, they were in no hurry.

Three miles later, they came to a place where two smaller creeks came together to make a larger one. There was a small meadow to one side, and the tracks showed an abundance of animal activity.

"This looks like a good spot," Zane said, surveying the area. "We can set up back from the meadow. Maybe you guys could pick up a careless rabbit or a raccoon this evening."

Ty got another burst of energy. "I'm going to look around. You want to come, Joseph?"

"Do you want to set up camp now, Dad?" Joseph asked.

"I'll do it. You guys go ahead. Don't go far, though. Use the creek as a landmark. Stick together, understand, Ty?"

"Okay, Dad," Ty didn't mind staying with Joseph. He didn't really feel like he had to. He would be okay, but if Dad said so, he would listen. He learned a long time ago to mind his father when they were out in the woods. Out here there were no arguments.

It was a muggy afternoon. Clouds still passed overhead, occasionally leaving an opening long enough for the sun to warm the forest floor.

Joseph and Ty walked a slow tour of the area. After a few minutes, Ty excitedly pointed at a doe with her spotted fawn. The deer trotted through the trees, anxious to put some distance between them and these new predators. Joseph and Ty were constantly astonished at the abundance of deer and other animal tracks.

"Man, this place is loaded with game. If Dad would let us shoot a deer, we could get one easy," Ty said.

"Yeah, you're right about that. Look at this trail. It's like a freeway."

"Why do you think Dad won't let us shoot a deer? No one would know. We could leave the skin and make jerky out of the meat. And I would love a great big deer steak right now."

"I think it would be too easy," Joseph answered. "It would be pretty hard to concentrate on survival skills if we had twenty pounds of jerky tied to our backs."

"Yeah, I guess you're right. It'd be pretty cool, though. Go out on a survival trip, make a bow, and get a deer and everything."

Ty thought about the glory of life while they circled around, crossed another creek, and then worked their way back up the other side.

As they went, Joseph thought about the day. It had been like walking through Eden, with flowers and trees, birds and animals untouched by man.

How could people think they could improve on this by pouring concrete on it? Joseph wondered as he watched his brother creep within shooting-distance of a couple of pine squirrels.

When they got back, Zane was completing a second fish trap. The traps were similar to the ones they had used before. Zane took off his shoes and waded awkwardly across the slippery rocks. After a few minutes, he managed to anchor the traps at the bottom of a couple of small eddies. Satisfied his traps would not wash away, Zane sat with his sons beside the rambling stream.

"It would be nice if we could spend enough time to get to know this valley, wouldn't it, boys?"

"It sure would," Ty responded eagerly.

"Do you think people get in here very often, Dad?" Joseph asked.

"I doubt it. There are probably a couple of trails crossing through; most people probably stick to them, so they won't get lost. I would guess that not more than a few people a year would have a chance to see the country that we've seen. You never know, though. We could walk all the way out without seeing another human track. Or we could run into a couple of groups of backpackers."

"I would hate to see other hikers out here," Ty said.

"Then what you have to do is see them before they see you. If they don't see you, it can add to the game."

"Cool," Ty said, smiling at the idea of sneaking around a group of backpackers.

"We better set up a lean-to tonight," Zane said. "I can't tell if it's going to rain or not."

"It has been a pretty cool day, hasn't it, Dad?" Joseph asked.

"It sure has, son. Every time I look out around me, it looks like God is reaching a hundred arrows of golden light down through the clouds to warm the earth."

Joseph thought about God's gifts to this valley. Ty imagined squirrels basking in the glow as the sun broke through the clouds.

"It is still a few hours until dark, but I'm going to start setting up camp. You guys can help or kick back. Do whatever you want."

"Where do you want to set it up?" Joseph asked.

"Over there looks good to me. It's far enough from the water so we can hear what is going on around camp, and I think it will be far enough away from the meadow that we won't disturb the locals."

Ty flashed his always ready smile. "That sounds good to me. I'm going to wait until one of those locals pokes its little nose out, and I'm going to slam him and eat him."

"Sitting in a ground stand would be good practice for you, Ty. It was my hardest lesson as a young man."

"I got that squirrel from a ground stand the other day," Ty said with youthful pride.

"Yeah, you sure did."

Zane and his sons went over to start to work on the lean-to. It was a familiar job. Within an hour and a half, the reasonably watertight shelter and the bedding area were situated. A safe distance away, they arranged a fire ring and broke branches in anticipation of an evening fire.

It was starting to cool off in the valley. The clouds grew thicker, so the warmth of the day remained near the earth. The sun retreated far to the west, now hanging over the distant mountains.

"Well, boys, I haven't had my bath yet today. I believe I'll take care of that right now. Why don't you guys see if you can hunt us up some food?"

Zane headed down to the creek while the boys circled around to the far side of the meadow. After a close check of the trails next to the creek where a raccoon had been making recent visits, the boys started looking for good places to sit and watch.

"This looks good to me," Ty said, walking into the middle of a group of young fir trees.

"Okay, I'll go a little farther. When I get to my spot, I'll whistle. You whistle back, so I'll know that you know where I am."

Ty nodded, and Joseph quietly snuck off to find a hiding place. A few minutes later, Ty heard Joseph's best bird call, and he returned his own.

A few minutes after full dark the boys stumbled back into camp. They had been glad to see the blazing fire in the dark to help guide them home. Over the fire their father was roasting a nice jackrabbit.

"How did you guys do?"

"Not as good as you. I had two shots at rabbits. On one, I was so close it jumped over backward," Joseph responded.

"I saw one rabbit and six deer. I didn't get a good shot at the rabbit."

"Well, one of you can take charge of this one while I put the finishing touches to my bow. Then all I'll need is a string."

Zane woke up with his spear in his hand. A thick fog hung over the valley. He pulled his feet beneath him. Hunkering under the lean-to, he listened. All he heard was the falling of the creek through the dense quiet.

"It's time to get up, guys."

Joseph and Ty pulled themselves together in the damp air.

"Boy, it sure is foggy," Ty said, rubbing his eyes.

"Yeah, it is," Joseph agreed with apprehension in his voice.

"Gather your things, boys. I'll check the fish."

Fifteen minutes later Zane returned with four brook trout. Immediately, he began the task of cooking up the pink spotted fish.

"All right! Fish for breakfast!" Ty said, excited at the prospect.

"Sounds good to me," Joseph said, warming his hands at the fire.

"You take care of these, Ty. I want to get going as soon as possible."

Zane and Joseph quickly dismantled the camp. Ty finished cooking the fish and started eating. Zane and Joseph finished their job and wolfed down the remaining fish. After scattering the rocks from the fire ring and burying the extinguished coals, the three rugged-looking hunters were off. Zane cradled his spear in his hand, and Joseph and Ty trotted behind with their bows still in their quivers.

Twenty-Three

It arrived at full light, mired in heavy fog and giving the day a feeling of timelessness. Joseph and Ty followed their father, content to look at his back. Their clear vision extended only twenty feet to each side.

This forty-foot circle of vision moved along with them as they traversed the valley. Seeing only a small bit of forest at any time, everything looked the same. For all the boys knew, their father was walking them around and around their camp.

Zane walked at a strong pace. Like a man late for an appointment, he pressed the fog. The boys hurried to keep up. A thousand years of proud heritage propelled Zane across the forest floor. He had never considered his own survival in the wilderness. He walked the earth like the coyote he wore on his back, fierce in battle, relentless in the protection of his tribe, and never asking more from this world than this day's food.

Zane pushed forward with a sense of urgency. He didn't know where he was going, not even certain about his direction. He sensed his mind didn't need to know. His feet carried him now, propelled forward like they had walked this path many times before. His palms felt sweaty as he gripped his spear. He desperately hoped that he would be on time. But for what, he did not know.

Zane glanced back at his sons. He saw no tiredness in their eyes, only a puzzled "why are we in such a hurry" look.

"Let's go, boys. We can't slow yet."

Zane and his sons gained the crest of a low ridge. Instead of dropping into another valley, the ground plateaued flat like a tabletop. The timber continued for about thirty yards straight ahead of them. The fog turned into a wispy white. At the edge of the aspen grove, Zane watched as the light breeze slowly cleared the fog from their side of the meadow. Looking into the translucency of the wispy clouds, Zane saw a dark mound in the grass before them. His spine tingled and the muscles in his chest and stomach braced in anxious anticipation.

"String your bows and knock an arrow," Zane said to his two sons, who stood firmly beside him.

Joseph and Ty could feel the seriousness in their father's voice. They had felt it for the last hour. There had been no hesitation in their walk, and there was no hesitation now. Without saying a word or making a sound, both boys strung their bows and knocked their best arrows.

"Let's see what calls us," Zane said, stepping from the fog into the mist that filled the meadow.

Joseph felt the world thick around him. The air seemed fresher than he had ever remembered. His muscles felt strong and hard. He walked behind a man that all his life he had dreamed of being like. At this moment, he felt the strength of the Nez Perce Nation come upon him. Today, he was a Nez Perce warrior.

Zane and his sons approached the animal lying in the grass. As they drew nearer, Zane could see what it was, but not until he stood over their fallen cousin could he see what its fate had been. It was an old mule deer that had fallen victim to the winter. Until recently, it had been covered with snow. Now the warmth of spring freed it from its frozen grave. The warm sun-of-spring did more than warm the ground and melt the snow. It also brought forth hungry animals from their long winter sleep.

Zane counted tracks of three of these animals here. Three black bears had been feeding on the carcass. Two of them had fed a couple of days earlier. The third much larger bear had fed earlier today, maybe even within the last hour.

Zane looked around them, then back in the direction from which they had come.

He saw the largest black bear he had ever seen. It was huge. It must have heard them coming up through the aspens and circled around behind them. Now, they were at his kill.

Zane could see the bear's lips curl and hear a hollow popping of his jaw. He could feel the pounding of the bear's feet on the earth as it approached. Never had he seen this kind of blood lust in the eyes of a wild animal. He had no doubt this bear meant to kill them all, simply for the pleasure of killing.

The bear approached at a steady, unrelenting pace. He was in no hurry. The panic of the prey was half the pleasure. For a long time, he had hunted man and animal. He knew there was no escape for them.

"Listen carefully, boys. We are going to have to kill this bear. We are Nez Perce warriors. He is no match for us. Back up with me as I talk. Move slowly and don't look at his eyes. Stay behind me and to the side enough for a clean shot when I hit him."

Zane backed slowly into the meadow. His eyes never left the bear's. He wanted the bear to want him first. If he looked to check on one of his sons, the bear might see them as a better target.

The bear closed the gap. Continuing steadily, he waited for one of his opponents to break and run, so he could take them in a charge. But these three men did not run.

He had seen the one in the middle many years before when he was a boy. He would be first. He would crush this man's skull. The one to left of the man was a boy. To get to him, he would have to pass the man. The one to his right was a man in the body of a boy, a secondary threat to be dealt with today, as well.

The bear, now only fifteen yards away, could cover that distance in a heartbeat.

"His heart is four inches above dead center," Zane said in a low voice. "I'll take his charge. Don't shoot until I hit him. Then empty your quivers. If you run, he'll kill you. Together, we can eat him for dinner."

Zane planted his feet and checked his knife. The three stood ready, each afraid for a different reason. They all feared this bear, but they would not run. They would stand and fight together.

With a deafening roar, the black bear with a silver face rose to his hind legs. His seven hundred-fifty pounds of primal rage lunged forward with the speed of a racehorse.

Zane screamed a war cry and gave a short, low step forward.

The bear saw Zane leap toward him and lay his weapon into the tall grass. The veteran of a hundred mortal duels stared into Zane's eyes. He raised his massive front legs, and then with one last thrust of his powerful haunches, he hurled himself at the man's head.

The bear crossed the meadow with frightening speed. Zane laid his spear low to encourage a direct charge. In a fight to the death that lasts only a couple of seconds, there is no thought. Only instinct preserves life.

The bear in his last stride rose slightly to hit Zane with a one-two smash from his huge club-like paws. As the bear lifted, Zane rocked backward, planting the butt of his spear in the dirt and resting the point of the spear in the center of the giant bear's chest.

The roar turned to a scream as the bear's momentum drove the point deeper and deeper beyond the heavy muscles into his center. In the same instant, blood lust turned to fear and then to rage. With his powerful left paw, the bear shattered the shaft of the spear into fragments, shifting the spear point in an arc in his chest, and slicing everything within. Another deafening roar, screaming with hatred beyond anything he had ever known, he flew again at his opponent.

Zane stumbled backward, trying to keep his footing. The great animal stalled for an instant, then it lurched forward. Zane drove his knife into the massive neck of the bear. Seeing all things now in slow motion, Zane looked to his left and saw the massive, clawed paw of the bear coming for his head. He desperately tried to move, but his body failed to respond.

He looked back to the mouth of the bear. His jaw gaped open to display his horrible flesh-tearing teeth and a mouth full of blood. The bear's paw smashed across Zane's left shoulder, then pounded the left side of his head, lifting him into the air. He looked at his son Joseph, who reached for another arrow to shoot at his attacker.

I have fine sons, Zane thought as he collapsed into a bloody heap on the soft spring meadow.

TWENTY-FOUR

When Zane regained consciousness, a woman about his age knelt over him. Her long black braids touched his chest as she examined his battered shoulder. Piercing pain stabbed into him at both his shoulder and his forehead. He lay motionless and silent as the woman completed her examination.

She wore a beautifully made and decorated doeskin dress. The beading and designs showed her to be a person of wealth and power in the tribe. Her style of clothing also revealed her Nez Perce origins.

As her skillful hands surveyed his wounds, she recited a chant that Zane had never heard before. A cool bandage covered the left side of his head, including his eye. His right eye was uncovered and the more it examined this woman, the more intriguing she became. Her dress was not only beautifully made, but it was sewn with real sinew and finely cut leather, not the synthetic sinew that he and everyone else he knew now used.

Her clothes showed very little mixture with other tribes, although she wore a Shoshone belt and a Flathead necklace. Both were extraordinarily well-made. Items of this quality were not sold. They were either gifts or made yourself if you were one of the very few people who still possessed such great skill.

"What is your name?" Zane asked in Nez Perce.

"My name is Willow Woman. I have work to do now. Talk to me later."

Through the pain, Zane turned his ears to what was happening around him. For the first time he realized the chaos surrounding him as people ran and screamed all around him. With enormous effort, he turned his head to gain a better view.

Men, women, and children ran everywhere. Women and children dropped to their knees and cried over the dead and wounded. Some lay motionless where they had fallen, their heads red from the lack of hair.

Zane registered that he was in an ancient Nez Perce village recovering from an enemy attack.

Willow Woman finished her examination. Rocking back onto her knees, she finished her chanting while shaking an ornately adorned fan of Bald Eagle feathers over him. Then, silent and motionless, she sat as if in solemn prayer. Suddenly finished, she looked at Zane.

"Do you have questions for me? I have other people to care for."

"Where am I? And where are my sons?"

"You are in the village of Chief Rolling Thunder. Porcupine Man brought you here when the Bannock attacked. You killed their War Chief, and he almost killed you. I know nothing of your sons. They are not here. We can talk more later."

The woman stood up and hurried off to minister to another casualty.

"I killed their War Chief? Porcupine Man brought me?" Zane tried to sit up, but the pain was severe.

"Do not move so much. You need to lie still."

Zane turned his head to see who belonged to this soft but commanding voice. Kneeling next to him to his left was the most beautiful woman he had ever seen. She was about twenty years old. As elegant as a queen, her eyes showed wisdom Zane had never seen in a person so young. Her long black braids rested over her shoulders and hung down to her waist.

"Who are you?" Zane asked.

"I am Spring. Chief Many Scars was almost upon me when you appeared. He fell at your feet with your spear in his heart. You saved my family and me. Chief Many Scars would surely have killed us all. I hope Raven pecks off his private parts before his spirit finds another home. You rest now."

Zane reluctantly closed his weary eyes. When he awoke, it was late afternoon. He was lying in a tepee on a buffalo skin. A soft elk hide blanketed him. Around him were the belongings of a powerful warrior and his family. Next to the center fire were two beds with room for three more. Those three were rolled up and stacked to one side.

There was an area where the women worked, and a place set aside for the storage and drying of various plants. Next to this were the man's weapons, all brilliantly decorated with golden eagle feathers and weavings. Zane heard a woman wailing and a horse galloped close by the tepee. As he sat up, pain washed across him. When the pain became tolerable, he struggled to his feet. He wanted to see what was happening outside.

Stepping into the bright clear afternoon, he took his first real look at the village.

He stood near the edge of a gathering of about seventy to eighty tepees. Men, women, and children all moved around. Drums pounded and dogs barked. Outside of a couple of the tepees, he saw women cutting their hair and slashing their forearms while wailing for their dead.

A few of the older men talked to a group of braves. Most of them wore war paint. Other men had stripped to their breech clouts and painted themselves as young boys watched. Foreheads were painted red or orange. A red stripe went down the center part of their hair. Other symbols were painted in red, orange, yellow, and black on the rest of the warrior's bodies and faces.

Horses were painted to match the riders. Some of the horses had white handprints on their sides.

Zane heard the screams of a man from the other side of camp. People paid little attention to Zane as he made his way through the excitement toward the screams. Near the middle of camp, a man stood with his feet tied to stakes in the ground. One arm was tied behind his back and the other held up a pole with four human scalps attached.

A group of women danced around him, tormenting him and jabbing him with sharp sticks. Whenever he set down the pole, the women stabbed him viciously until he raised it again. Blood poured from his back, chest, and sides. From his war paint, Zane could tell the man was Bannock.

So it goes, Zane thought.

He heard the thunder of hooves and turned away from the frantic, bloody dance. A large group of mounted men came into camp. Flatheads. Zane had met Flatheads at powwows, but he had only seen pictures of why they received their name. The self-imposed deformity gave them a terrifying appearance. The women and children stayed clear of the fierce horsemen, but they did not run, either.

Some of the older braves and chiefs went to greet them and Zane wandered over to close enough to hear what was being said.

"Hello, my friends. You are always welcome in my camp. Thank you for coming."

"Hello, Chief Rolling Thunder. I am sorry we meet again under such circumstances."

"Yes, Chief Red Cloud. It is a sad day when the Bannock break a truce that has lasted for so many lifetimes. Come, let us sit and talk."

Rolling Thunder took Red Cloud and his twenty Flathead braves to the place where he had been speaking to his men earlier. They sat in a circle, sometimes three or four deep. Zane estimated there to be over one hundred fighting men.

Zane found it hard to contain his excitement. He sat at the

edge of the circle of braves, hoping he was close enough to hear the Chiefs words. As he settled in, the warriors around him smiled or nodded their approval, then refocused their attention on the Chiefs.

"For many lifetimes we have had a spring and early summer truce with the tribes of the south and the east. The Nez Perce, Flatheads, Piute, Shoshone, and the Bannock have kept this time apart for peaceful travel and trade. It is a time to talk and to exchange ideas and goods, and for all to replenish our food supplies. It is our time to become strong as nations. It is a time for harmony in the world.

"This morning, while Chief Running Dog and thirty of our men hunted for food, the Bannock War Chief Many Scars attacked our camp. Many of our people would have died today, but Porcupine Man brought a great warrior from the other side. This man stood alone as the enemy came out of the mist. He attacked them and slew the Bannock's greatest War Chief Many Scars. The alarm was sounded, and our braves drove the enemy from our camp. If this man had not come to our aid, many of us would be crying for our lost children."

Rolling Thunder stood. "Stand, my friend."

The braves around Zane looked at him and motioned for him to stand. He pushed up to his feet and looked from face to face. Zane knew that one day he would ride into battle beside these men. There was a bond here as strong as his love for his sons. These were his people.

"From this day on, you will be called Stands in the Mist. This camp is your home for as long as you wish."

Zane smiled and nodded his approval. Rolling Thunder sat down, as did Zane. The braves around him slapped him on the back, sending shockwaves of pain through his shoulder. They reached back, congratulating him, and invited him to move to the innermost circle. These braves sitting beside him now were as friendly but less impressed. They were the strongest and the most courageous. If they had been lucky enough to have been there, they would have killed Many Scars, too.

"When the Bannock were driven from our camp, I sent two men to follow them. They will return tonight and lead us to the enemy."

A man sitting two places to the right of Chief Rolling Thunder spoke next.

"I am Chief Running Dog. I have fought Many Scars band many times. He has a son. His name is Sits on a Ridge and Waits. He will be leading them now. I have watched him, and I have fought him. He will run, leaving a trail for us to follow. Then he will wait to ambush us. I would like to lead the attack against him."

Rolling Thunder spoke again. "This morning Many Scars attacked from the South. He fell at the door of Chief Running Dog's tepee. Two years ago, Chief Running Dog killed Many Scars oldest son in battle. I think Many Scars wanted revenge on Chief Running Dog. It is right that he leads this war party. But if you do not catch them before they reach Shoshone country, let them go. We do not want a fight with the Shoshone."

Chief Red Cloud spoke next. "For many lifetimes the Nez Perce and the Flathead have been friends. I also have fought Many Scars. The Bannock are truly an enemy to be fought. They must know this time that what has always been a time of truce must be honored. My men and I will go with Chief Running Dog. We will take many scalps, and the Bannock will know that The One Above Us All will not allow the Bannock to break the harmony of our world."

The chiefs and many braves nodded at this wisdom. They knew that Hunyawat would control the field of battle. Why else would Porcupine Man have chosen sides? Was he not a teacher and a creator for the Bannock, as well?

From the evening until late in the night, there was feasting and dancing. The chiefs and fathers prepared the younger and less experienced braves for battle. Men told stories of past raids. There were tales of great heroism. The young men were eager to be counted amongst the warriors of future raids. The women cooked deer and elk over their fires. The men prepared their horses and weapons for the first battle of the year.

Zane stayed at the edge of the excitement. This was all new to him. At the same time, he felt like he had done this all before. He watched Spring, Willow Woman, and the other women prepare the food and see to the needs of their men.

The Flatheads stayed somewhat to themselves, even though they were treated as honored guests. Some had friends in this camp, who invited them over to talk or to join in the dance.

"Why don't you join them, Stands in the Mist?" Spring asked, startling Zane out of deep thought.

"Not now. Spring, did I die?"

"Porcupine Man brought you to fight Many Scars. I heard him and my mother talking. He said that you are special. He said that when you are healed, you may return to where you came from. I have never heard of someone coming from the other side and going back. Porcupine Man is a very powerful Wyakin, but I did not think he could do this."

"Do you know if my sons are all right?"

"They did not pass this way. While you are here, the other side is not your concern. You told us you slew a great bear. If they are your sons, they will be fine. My mother is the most powerful healer in the Nez Pearce nation. She understands these things better than any other person in our village. Maybe she can answer your questions.

"Coyote said that he would explain it to me once. But he said that I had to lie naked on his fur bed and it would come to me in a dream. He thinks that he is so sly. I should put Many Scars in his bed. Coyote would probably not know the difference."

Zane and Spring laughed at the macabre joke.

"My father is Chief Running Dog. He will want to thank you for saving me and my sister and brother. You should talk to him."

"I have not yet thanked you and Willow Woman for ministering to me."

"There are no thanks needed. I must go now," Spring said, smiling broadly as she left.

There was so much that Zane did not understand, but he knew that he would get no answers tonight. The least he could do was thank his host for his hospitality. Zane found Chief Running Dog going over strategy with the other chiefs. As he walked near, Running Dog saw him and stood.

"Come here, my friend, and sit with us. This man saved my family and slew my enemy today. For this, I am always in your debt. I live that one day I may stand in the gap for your family. Sit here with us."

Zane was greeted all around. They had all seen Many Scars in battle. Any man who could defeat him hand to hand was worthy to sit with them.

The men who had followed the Bannock war party returned. They had watched the group of about forty braves camp twenty miles to the south. Zane listened as these veterans of many battles decided where the enemy might spring their ambush. When all the preparations had been made, Chief Running Dog gave the command to mount. Sixty fighting men, including the twenty Flatheads, slipped quietly into the night air.

Zane found Willow Woman organizing the camp clean-up.

"Willow Woman, I would like to talk with you."

"We can talk tomorrow morning. Tonight, you may sleep in my husband's tepee."

He knew better than to force the question. He thanked her for the hospitality and went back to the lodge where he had slept earlier. Inside, Spring and two children already slept. He looked through the shadows of his host's home. If it didn't hurt so much, he would think it to be the most bizarre dream. Finally, Zane gratefully crawled under the warm, elk skin robe.

As he awoke, Zane looked up to a movement above him. In the upper reaches of the tepee, a wide fan of Bald Eagle feathers seemed to dance with the sunlight to the breeze that drifted up to the smoke hole at the top. It was like a bird silently keeping watch, with the shadow and light reflecting off the tail feathers casting about the floor below. From dream to reality, Zane moved his head carefully side to side to see if he was alone in the room.

"Are you awake?"

Zane turned to see Walker, Spring's ten-year-old brother, looking through the door of the tepee. "I'm awake," he answered.

"My sister has food for you."

Zane carefully rolled up from his side and stepped into a sparkling cool morning. Spring handed Zane a small tightly woven bowl that was full of greens and a piece of grilled meat. Most were food that he had eaten before apart from a large tuber. He would remember to ask what the plant looked like and where it grew.

"You must eat to regain your strength."

Zane gratefully took the food and sat down to eat.

"My father also wanted you to have this." Spring handed Zane a beautiful obsidian knife with a wrapped rawhide handle, complete with a scabbard and belt. He looked at it, not knowing how to accept such a gift. Then he looked to his side and, for the first time, realized that his knife and belt were missing. He saw too that his clothes were sewn with sinew. There was nothing on him that could not have come from this camp.

"My father said that a warrior should not be without a knife."

"I will thank him when I see him," Zane said, tying it around his waist.

"You are healing very quickly but my mother said that you are to remain quiet for a few days. If you like, I can help you trade for a bow. It will give you something to do so I won't have to constantly be telling you to move slowly and rest."

Together, Zane and Spring wended their way through the village looking for the tool maker. The old man sat in front of his tepee. A deerskin was laid out beside him with flint and obsidian arrow points. There were groups of points, rough to finished, spread across it. A portion of the skin was draped over his leg, and he was shaping a point that was tucked firmly into his left hand.

He worked the edge of the stone with a measured quickness. Zane and Spring stood before the man without speaking, waiting for him to finish his work on the stone. In a few moments, he worked a rough flake into a beautifully balanced, razor-sharp, large game hunting point. Zane could see that this man was truly a master tool maker. The old man examined his work, then placed it onto the hide with the other completed points.

"Spring, your father gives our new friend the knife that I made for him. What is it that you want me to give to him?"

"Now Yellow Wood, you greet me this way. Are you taking the cure every day as I told you?"

"Yes, I eat the bitter weeds. I think that they are the wrong cure. They make my food taste bad. Do you see how I am getting thinner?"

"Has the pain in your chest gone away?"

"Yes, I have no more pain, except for the hunger in my stomach because my food does not taste good any longer. Now I eat only twice each day! Soon I will have the frame of a child. I have lived more winters than I can count. I have earned the right to be a fat old man!"

"Now Yellow Wood, you will never have the frame of a child. And it is not good for you to eat too much. However, if you are hungry, I know how you can get all the venison that you want for one full moon. Stands in the Mist is a fine hunter, but he has no bow or arrows. If you could provide these, then he would provide you with four fine young deer over the next moon."

"I will do this if you give me a cure for my pain that does not change the taste of my food . . . so much."

"Good then, we have an agreement."

"Stands in the Mist, be careful of this girl. She is wiser than her years, and she gives a man no peace. You may take these. I made them for myself. You can find none better. Good hunting."

Zane smiled and said, "I think that you give good counsel. This is a fine bow; it is a good trade for me."

Spring and Zane walked toward the center of camp, being greeted as they went by friendly smiles and casual conversation.

"Stands in the Mist, I think that you are well enough to try your new bow." Spring untied a leather pouch from her waist and handed it to Zane. "Here is a little bit of pemmican and some herbs. The herbs are for pain and to help your blood. Take them all when you eat the food."

"Spring, you have been so kind to me. I don't know how I can repay you."

"I am a healer. Caring for people is what I do. But if you like, you may find a way to repay me."

Spring left Zane with a smile that caused his heart to rumble in his chest. As he watched her leave, a soft warm glow rolled from his toes up through his body till it flew from the ends of his black hair as it tossed in the gentle breeze. Stands in the Mist watched while the beautiful young healer went to care for her other patients.

TWENTY-FIVE

In his recent memory he had only traveled this trail one time, but his recollection of the area blossomed beyond memory. He had been here before. Each trail carried visions. Every tree and clearing that he passed left him with re-lived moments of forgotten times.

Lifetimes of hunts and hikes swept before him as his legs carried him through the forest. The strength that fortifies a man when he lives in the magic, knowledge, and wisdom of the world swelled within him. He saw, and he remembered. He watched and he listened; his legs carried him till he found himself in the clearing near where he and his sons had spent their last camp together. Zane half-walked, half-staggered into the clearing. He fell to his knees and wept with his face in his hands.

"Why is it that the strongest men weep this way?"

Zane looked up and leapt to his feet. Twenty feet in front of him was a man who was not a man. As Zane watched him, the creature rested down onto his front feet and flared his quills, then rested them again low onto his back.

"Why do you think it is so?" Porcupine Man asked again.

"I do not know if it is so."

"Why do you weep, Zane Carter?"

"How can a man live without his sons?"

"You have the strength of your ancestors. Your brothers and their sons are all around you. You possess the power of the ancients. But I knew that you would not rest. Hunyawat has something more for you to do. It isn't time for you to live with your ancestors? That does leave me with a problem, though. What shall I tell her? You know that she will ask."

Zane smiled, then felt sadness. "Tell her, does the world around you know how softly your branches greet the air? How gently you comfort the fledgling nest. From spring to spring, I will hold you gently in my heart till I see you again."

Zane slowly opened his eyes. The first morning rays reached out into the trees. A rough lean-to cast a dark shadow over him. His head was wrapped tight with the gauze that he had carried for ten years in his emergency first aid kit. His head and neck felt like they had been hit with an axe and his mouth was as dry as desert sage. Starting by wiggling his toes, he did a check for pain and problems. Working his way up his body, he decided that his shoulder and his head were his only injuries.

A smile spread across his face when he realized the weight covering him was a huge black bear's skin. *One of my boys alone couldn't have skinned a bear this size.*

"My sons are all right," Zane said with an overwhelming sigh of relief. Relaxing his weary muscles, a weight fell from his shoulders and back. He didn't have to be strong now. His boys were alive. There was no danger for them now. They were Nez Perce braves. They would take care of him.

Zane looked out toward the trees and saw Joseph and Ty carrying armloads of wood back to the lean-to. As they got closer, Zane saw the already large piles of wood in the meadow.

"No!" Zane yelled as loud as he could, the pain wrenching his skull. "It's Dad!" Ty yelled, dropping his branches and sprinting for the lean-to.

"Dad, you're alive?" Joseph yelled, gaining on Ty.

Ty tumbled down and hugged his father, sending a shockwave of pain across Zane's smiling face.

"I thought you were dead," Ty said with his eyes full of tears.

"We both did," Joseph said, sobbing and hugging his father over the top of Ty.

"You guys are killing me," Zane groaned, not wanting to stop his sons but unable to endure the pain.

Joseph realized they were lying on their father and shifted to a spot beside him. "Ty, he's still hurt."

Ty lifted his head from his father's chest, knowing he should move but not wanting to pull away.

"Sorry, Dad," Ty said, moving back just enough to be not quite touching.

"How do you feel? Can I get you anything?" Ty asked.

"I'm thirsty."

Ty looked at Joseph, not knowing how he could carry a drink to his father.

"Take the raccoon skin and hold it like a bowl. That should carry enough," Joseph instructed. Since the morning before, when their father had been injured, Joseph had been in charge. Ty instantly obeyed him and took off running in the direction of the creek.

"Don't light the signal fire. I'll be okay," Zane said, looking at his older son.

"Are you sure, Dad? You have been out since yesterday."

"I'll be fine. I need a day or two to rest. You and Ty weren't hurt?"

"No, Dad," Joseph said. "You killed him. We both shot all our arrows into him. But you cut his heart and both lungs with your spear. Then you cut his throat with your knife. After he hit you, he just stood there getting hit by arrows until he fell. We wrapped your head and covered you up. Then we thought you were dead. Ty didn't stop crying for hours. I didn't start a signal fire yesterday because it was so foggy. I didn't think it would help. Man, I'm glad you're not dead."

Joseph gave his father another hug as gently as he could.

"Well, we have enough food to last us a while. That bear was a giant. Ty and I couldn't even roll him over. We had to skin his legs and cut them off. Then just keep going until we had the hide off him."

"Where is he?" Zane asked, looking around.

"He is on the other side of the lean-to. It looks like we skinned a big fat man and left parts lying around. It's really creepy. I was worried about Ty. He keeps going over and looking at it, then sits next to you and cries. Man, I am glad you're okay."

"Build a drying rack and dry a bunch of the meat. You must cook it well before you dry it. Bear meat has bad bugs if you don't cook it. It is going to take me a few days before I can walk out. I'm proud of you, Joseph. You're a wonderful son. You did a great job of taking care of me and Ty," Zane said. Then he leaned forward with tears in his eyes, took Joseph's hand and said, "Joseph, I saw them. I was there."

Ty came running up the hill as fast as he could and still keep some of the water in the skin. "Here you go, Dad."

Zane gratefully drank the water then laid his head back onto the soft pillow of fur.

"I'm going to get some sleep now," Zane said, closing his eyes.

Joseph and Ty sat by his side, watching him breathe and grinning from ear to ear.

While Zane slept, Joseph and Ty cut the meat into thin strips, cooked it and hung it on drying racks. It was good to have something to do. Even Ty didn't feel like hunting or even moving too far from his father. The killing that had taken place the day before had given him a different perspective. Hunting was a way of life for him and his family. He wasn't going to stop. But after fighting the bear and almost losing his father, Ty would always possess a greater respect for the feelings of the other animals that his father called their cousins. Ty, having been an animal pursued for food, would never again pursue without feeling that fear and considering the responsibility of his actions.

Joseph was engrossed in different thoughts. He knew what his father had meant when he said, "I saw them; I was there." The words sent tingles up his back every time he repeated them to himself. But how did his father learn from the porcupine and the coyote? How was his father connected with the other animals?

He felt like he should understand, but he didn't. When he walked, he felt like he was on sacred ground, like he was being watched by friendly unseen eyes. There was a mystery here. The answer was all around him, but he could only see its shadows. He knew his father had visited the spirit world.

Joseph wasn't entirely convinced that his father had died. Never had Joseph wanted to know something as bad as he wanted to know this. What had happened to his father, and what had he seen? All his life he had heard the legends of his people. He felt that his father and some of the old people believed in at least part of them.

Joseph had always thought of them as stories, but there was something going on here. Joseph felt desperate to find out what it was. He was exhausted in the body but reeling with excitement in his mind. Something truly fantastic was happening here.

Zane slept through the day and the next night. Early the following morning before the sun rose, he sat up and stretched as best he could. His shoulder and neck still ached like hell. His head was all crusted with matted hair and dried blood. He felt the stabbing pain from the cut on the left side of his head. The bear skin covered the ground around him. "You were a great warrior, old man. It could easily have been me laying in pieces on the ground."

Zane carefully got to his feet. When he reached vertical, the world started to spin around him. Holding onto the side of the lean-to for support, he regained his balance. Then he smiled, feeling the rich morning air fill his lungs.

"It is a good day to be alive," Zane said to himself, carefully letting go and walking over to the drying racks for his first food in two days.

"How are you feeling, Dad?" Joseph asked, still lying under the bear skin.

"I feel good, and I feel injured. After I have a bite to eat, I would like to wash. Do you think you could help me with my bandages?"

Joseph liked being the doctor. If he had lived a century ago, he felt he would have been a healer. Joseph imagined himself in harmony with the natural world. With each passing minute, he felt that this life was his destiny.

Joseph hurried over to his father. Joseph and Ty had always seen him as the toughest man they had ever known. Sometimes out in the woods, he seemed to do things that could hardly even be believed. Joseph looked at his father this morning with a feeling of awe. Two days ago, his father had killed a seven-hundred-pound bear in hand-to-hand combat. As Joseph chewed a piece of blackened bear meat, he looked up at his father and a shiver ran up his back. One day he would be a man like his father.

"It is a beautiful morning, isn't it, son?" Zane said, chewing a tough piece of meat. "The old men say if you eat the first bear you kill, you will never kill another one. You know what, Joseph, I'm glad that it wasn't true for me!"

Zane and Joseph left Ty sleeping and walked down to the creek. Joseph had never seen his father move so slowly. About halfway down the short slope, Zane stopped and leaned against a tree.

"You okay, Dad?"

"I'll be fine if I take it easy today and again tomorrow. By then I should be back to peak condition," Zane said, smiling at his son. "You did a good job while I was gone. You cared for your brother, for me, and yourself. You are a man now, Joseph. At the next tribal meeting, I am going to tell everyone about your bravery and how you took care of us. Then you will be accepted as a man. You will be a man, equal to Tom and me and every other member of the tribe. When you speak, everyone will listen."

Joseph was overwhelmed at the thought. He had attended powwows with his father, but he had never stood before the tribal council. He had seen it but was never allowed to participate. The old men would sit around together, and the other men would sit around them in a large group. They would talk about problems and events. They would discuss plans for the future, and sometimes they would even tell stories from the past. It was a good time, a proud time, but it was a very serious time.

The thought of standing up and talking in front of all the important and powerful people in the tribe was more than Joseph wanted to think of right now. He would almost rather face that bear again. He knew that time would come though, and when it did, he would stand up. He would speak loud and clearly. He would make his father proud.

"Let's go get washed up," Joseph said, turning down the hill.

Zane followed his son. At the creek, Joseph carefully unwrapped the bandages. Zane knelt with his head next to the water. Joseph washed his father's hair and the cut area as best he could.

"It looks pretty good," Joseph said. "You are going to need a bunch of stitches, though. I wish I could put on fresh bandages."

"It feels pretty good. Any kind of head wound bleeds a lot. You did a good job. Have Ty bring down the first aid kit. Clean it again as thoroughly as you can. Then you and Ty use the rest of the disinfectant ointment before using duct tape to close the wound. You will need to dry the skin, get a good hold with the tape on one side then work together to pull and push the scalp together before laying down the tape across the other side. It will be difficult and messy, but you can do it."

After washing and closing the wound, they rewrapped it. Then cleaned up and went back up to camp.

After Zane laid down on the warm bear skin, Ty asked, "How are you feeling, Dad?"

"I feel okay, Ty. How about you?"

"All right. What do you want to do today?"

"We need to tan this skin. I need to get some more rest. If you broke arrows, you could gather more."

"Oh, man!" Ty said, not feeling like doing that kind of work anymore. "I'll get the arrow shafts!" he volunteered. At least that way he could walk around a bit. Maybe he would even see a rabbit to shoot. Then he thought another moment and felt he had better not shoot even if he could. They had plenty of meat.

"I don't mind working on the hide," Joseph said. He was glad to have the time with his father.

"If you are going to walk around alone, Ty, be sure you stay next to the creek, so you won't get lost. We would be hard pressed finding you if you took off in the wrong direction. And keep your bow strung. When we were at our last camp, I saw lion tracks. He probably wouldn't bother you, but you never know."

Ty thought about having to face a mountain lion alone and shuddered. "I will, Dad." *You bet I will,* he thought.

Joseph cut the long tendons from the legs of the bear, then laid them on the drying rack. Then he spread out the skin, flesh side up and carefully started to scrape the remaining bits of flesh and fascia that had been missed during the skinning. It was a much harder job now that it was partially dried.

Ty watched for a while, then headed out of camp to search for arrow shafts. They had each broken arrows when the bear had fallen. *I'd like to find about ten good ones,* Ty thought.

"Dad," Joseph began, still working the edges of the fur, "yesterday you said you saw them. That you were there."

"I said that? I don't remember." Zane paused for a long moment.

Joseph glanced at his father, about to say something when Zane spoke again. "I did see them, though. After the great bear hit me, I crossed over. I was in the heart of the Nez Perce Nation.

Some of the people wanted me to stay so I could ride and hunt with them. A powerful medicine woman healed me. I was given the choice of returning or staying in the Nation. But I wasn't ready for a life without you and Ty."

Joseph stared at his father with awe in his eyes. "This has been like a dream to me. I thought you had died and now you're back. I had a vision that came true. It seems like it should be so easy to understand, but I'm not sure I am ready for all of this."

After a few hours, Joseph finished the fleshing then prepared the brain and mashed it over the hide. He had to use it more sparingly than before, but it covered adequately for a field tanning. When they got back home, they would do a better job of tanning everything.

Ty had been gone for hours, but Zane wasn't worried. Ty could take care of himself. He was tough, and the last few days were sure to temper his decisions. He would be fine.

Zane and Joseph sat in the shade of the lean-to. Joseph had brought water for Zane to drink. They also ate some meat and greens he had gathered.

"There is so much I want to ask you. I don't know where to begin."

Zane met Joseph's gaze. "Son, I will tell you everything, and it will be too much. It is going to sound like a modern version of one of the old legends. It will have the feeling of a dream. There is so much I don't understand, but I'll tell you this. I know your gentle heart and how you feel about our forefathers and their way of life. If you let the spirits of the earth speak to you, then you will find the answers to your questions. This is sacred ground. Our ancestors are all around us. They are healing my wounds and strengthening our spirits. One day, you and I will live here with them, and we will hunt buffalo with my grandfather."

Joseph knew his father was right about one thing. He wasn't ready to know what had happened to his father. It was too much.

Ty trudged up over the rise of the plateau with a quiver full of sticks. "Man, I bet I walked ten miles." He plopped down next to his father. "But I got some great arrows. I'll show you." He pulled out a dozen potential arrow shafts. "These five are my best, and these other ones are okay. A couple of them we might not be able to straighten out. They looked better before I cut them. But look at this. I found two crow feathers."

Zane examined each shaft and arranged them in groups. "This is great, Ty. There are nine usable shafts here. That is a lot better than I had expected."

The boys worked as Zane watched. The late afternoon rolled past in pleasant distraction until he felt a wave of exhaustion drift over him and settled into the comfort of the bear skin bed.

As the morning sun warmed the camp, Zane's sons washed and wrung out the bear's skin. Then they made a fire beneath the wooden frame and smoked the hide, careful not to make so much smoke as to cause alarm from any distant fire watchers.

Zane tested the long tendons from the bear. Finding them still too wet to make a string for his bow, he left them on the rack. Considering the size of the pelt, he estimated it would weigh about seventy pounds when dried.

TWENTY-SIX

After two more days of rest and recovery, Zane and his sons resumed their journey. Joseph wore the coyote cape and carried Zane's bow and arrows in his quivers. Ty carried his usual things, including his raccoon cape and the furs they had gathered.

Zane draped the large bear skin over his shoulders. Legs dangling, it extended down past his knees on both sides. They walked at a casual but steady pace, resting more than they had on their previous hikes. Still, they covered ten miles by late afternoon.

They camped next to a large pool in a creek big enough to be called a river. Washing and splashing in the water, they knew that the end of their trip would soon become a reality. The water wasn't as cold as it had been two and a half weeks before, and the dark forest didn't seem nearly so sinister.

The three lay naked on the rocks at the edge of their swimming hole, soaking in the last rays of a radiant spring day.

"This was the best day of my life," Ty said, looking around him.

"Mine, too," said Zane.

"That goes for me, too," agreed Joseph.

The bear skin made sleeping twice as comfortable. The pine

boughs were adequate, but adequate doesn't even compare with the warmth of a winter bear blanket.

The next few days were a casual hike. Twice they crossed trails that had been used by people, and once they crossed a jeep road. The road still hadn't been used this year, but it was a road and a sure sign that they approached civilization.

Still the countryside had a feeling of wilderness. They had their privacy. Game remained plentiful. They saw deer at regular intervals. They even watched a small bear tear apart a log, looking for insects. Squirrels chattered, and birds announced their arrival or sang their tunes. From the time they left the place the boys had named "Bear Meadow," they left the bows unstrung in their quivers. The hunt was over for this trip. They had all they needed.

They took time to enjoy watching the wildlife around them as they played and foraged and courted their mates. It was spring, and spring carried special wonders. Zane and his sons enjoyed every minute of their homeward journey.

On the morning of their eighteenth day, Zane, Joseph, and Ty walked into the clearing by a large lake. It was the image of an alpine paradise. A quaking aspen grove shimmered green leaves in a gentle breeze on one side of the lake, spreading its mirrored image out across the lake, disappearing into a morning mist that clung to the far shoreline.

A deer and her two fawns browsed the edge of the meadow not sixty yards from where the three stood. Zane and his sons walked out into the dew-covered grass. The deer looked up at them and then trotted into the forest canopy. One hundred yards beyond where the deer had stood sat their Bronco.

They looked at the vehicle almost in disbelief. How could their truck get out here in the middle of nowhere? Then, like waking from a dream, their trip concluded.

Zane, Joseph and Ty, who looked out of place in the same meadow with a Ford truck, walked silently over to the edge of the lake.

Fish rose in the water, sending out expanding rings, increasing, disrupting, and adding to the sweet serenity of the moment.

"I want to get a giant chocolate milkshake," Ty said, grinning up at his father.

"That sounds good to me," Zane agreed, smiling at his younger son. "The keys are on the front tire."

Ty trotted off in the direction of the truck.

"What sounds good to you, Joseph?"

"It seems strange to step back into this other world. I'm not sure what sounds good to me right now."

"You have the rest of your life to figure that out. But right now, let's go and get Ty's milkshake."

About the Author

After high school, Aaron Anderson set out to see the world, embarking on adventures through North America, Europe, and North Africa. He enjoyed traveling as a bicyclist, motorcyclist, train passenger, and even as a hitchhiker, reveling in the excitement of the unknown.

At the age of twenty-two, Aaron returned to the U.S. and worked on oil rigs in Wyoming. He later became a carpenter and eventually a real estate appraiser. However, his true passions have always been writing, developing powerful friendships, and exploring new country.

During the 1980s he and his two sons hunted, hiked, and camped throughout the western states. Here, his love for the natural world and respect for Indigenous people prompted him to write his second novel, *Never Lost*.